*Obsession. . . .*

"Maggie? What are you thinking? Where are you?"

How could I tell her my fantasy? That, more than anything in the world, I wanted to be like her. To look like her, talk like her, walk like her, think like her. Even more, I wanted to become her. She was perfect! She knew about life. She knew about death. She had suffered.

How I envied her.

Other Point paperbacks
you will enjoy:

*The Lie*
by Laura Sonnenmark

*Until Whatever*
by Martha Humphreys

*I Can Hear the Mourning Dove*
by James Bennett

*Life Without Friends*
by Ellen Emerson White

*point*

# THE
# EMPTY SUMMER

## CARYL BROOKS

SCHOLASTIC INC.

New York Toronto London Auckland Sydney

ISBN 0-590-45864-7

12 11 10 9 8 7 6 5 4 3 2 1          7          5 6 7 8 9/9 0/0

Printed in the U.S.A.                                    01

*For my Family*

*To Robert Hirsch, Theron Raines, Florence Engel Randall,*
*Penelope Mortimer, Regina Griffin, and*
*Tonya Alicia Martin —*
*thank you.*

# THE
# EMPTY SUMMER

Dear Maggie,

We're flying to New York! I can't wait to see you! We'll have lunch at Giovanni's and talk. Lately, I'm so confused. I feel lonely and afraid but I'm not sure why. I've learnd that nothing stays the same but promise me, Maggie, you'll always be my freind.

xxxx yo yo ☺

P.S.   I'm on a new diet.
P.P.S.   What's so great about growing up?

# ONE

Suddenly, it's spring. Blue wildflowers spread across our front lawn. They grow fuller each year. Now, like an apron, they almost touch the crab apple tree. I wait for them to appear. I'm superstitious. If they're late, I panic and think I'll flunk my finals. The minute I see them, I smile. They are my promises for happiness.

I hear the *wrrrr* of the lawn mower. The gardener is early this year. I run outside. Is it a premonition? I'm too late. The wildflowers are crushed, broken stems buried between blades of freshly cut grass. *Wrrrr.* "No! No!" I cry, pointing to the wildflowers. The gardener doesn't speak English. "You've killed them! You've killed them!" I shout. His face crumples. He stares at me. Crazy girl, he's thinking. Crazy girl. I race into the kitchen where my mother is running cold water over her paintbrushes. "The blue wildflowers . . . they're gone. They're dead!" I begin to sob.

She takes me in her arms. "My darling," she says. "My darling," over and over again. Then she asks me if it's all right to phone my school and speak with the guidance department.


Dr. Woods, a young psychologist, has started a group. A group of girls like myself, who wear sneakers and tight faded jeans. A group of girls like myself, who are unhappy.

How can I explain what I'm feeling?

I need those lovely wildflowers. I want them growing on the front lawn the same way as last spring and the spring before and the one before that.

"Would you like to tell us about it?" asks Dr. Woods at our first meeting.

I shake my head. I'm afraid. It's safer to keep everything inside. No one will know except me.

"Sometimes a diary or journal helps. It's a way of getting it all out." She makes it sound like a virus. Intestinal flu, or something.

I look around at the circle of girls. What are they thinking?

Do they know that I'm terrified of a million things? The crawling ivy outside my window. The walk to school. The luncheonette at the foot of the hill. Undressing for gym. Madame la Guinière calling on me for the past participle of *être*. My parents. I imagine them in their bedroom. My mother: "I'm concerned about her. It seems extreme." My father: "Give it time. It's normal under the circumstances."

I'm close to my parents. I love you. We say that to

and try to control a wheeze. "There's nothing, absolutely nothing that I . . ."

I can't say another word.

Everyone is staring at me . . . waiting.


Last year, there was me, Margaret Gray. Maggie, for short. Fifteen, dying to be sixteen, with brown hair, blue eyes, a regular nose, and a mouth. Quite ordinary, I could have been anybody. Even my life was uneventful. "Someday, you're going to be a knockout!" my father often remarked. That was his way of trying to boost my confidence. How long, I wondered, would I have to wait for my "someday"?

But there was more than me. There was Kimberly Porter. She's the one who was special. Tanned all over, even between her fingers. Complexion so dewy that a Jacuzzi might have been sloshing around under skin and bones. Long blonde hair, blunt cut to flip. Narrow shoulders, fragile wrists, and unexpectedly full breasts. Her eyebrows were thick, winging upward above pale green eyes. She was curved into one color, gold as honey poured from a pitcher.

My friend YoYo introduced us. YoYo and I were having lunch at Giovanni's in the Village. "I invited Kimberley," she said, reaching for a bread stick and then changing her mind. YoYo was round, made up of circles. Her face was soft and plump as a freshly baked muffin. Her dark hair was cut too short and she wore a red baggy sweater with sleeves pushed up to dimpled elbows. She carried her own American Express card and lived with her parents in Los Angeles. Her father was president of Pyramid Movie Productions. Her mother stayed at home. They visited New York every spring and stayed at The Pierre. In the evenings they held screenings of first-run films for all their friends. YoYo and her parents had a lot of friends. "You'll love Kimberley! She's great!" YoYo used the word *great* all the time.

"You've been going on and on about her for years," I said. "She sounds like a bore." The truth was that I didn't want to share YoYo with anyone. Who needs to hear that she's a part-time model with all A's in school? Beautiful *and* smart! What a disgusting combination.

"I have a feeling you'd be great friends."

"I'm not pretty enough and my I.Q. is only average. What would we have to talk about?"

"Maybe you're jealous because she's on the cover of *Seventeen*." YoYo knew me very well. Why not? We'd been friends ever since we were nine years old and were in the same bunk at camp.

"Which issue?" Not the latest? The one I grabbed off the newsstand because the cover girl was so breathtaking that for days I sucked in my cheeks to make them hollow as hers. Is that the one and only Kimberley? *Not* saying that I'd suspected it all along from having heard so much about her.

"Hi!" A daffodil brushed past me. All I saw was thin and yellow.

"Kimberley, I'd like you to meet Maggie Gray. Maggie, this is Kimberley Porter." YoYo never stumbled over introductions. She practiced at Hollywood parties.

Whoopi, this is Jason Priestley. Jason, I'd like you to meet Whoopi Goldberg.

"Hi!" breathed the daffodil once again, this time dazzling me with her smile. She carried a huge hobo pocketbook that she dropped onto the floor.

My imagination X-rayed its contents. Moisturizer. Eyeliner. Mascara. Taupe eye shadow. Plum blusher. Lip gloss. Q-tips. Magnifying mirror. Curling iron. Panty hose. Body stocking. Shoes. Scarf. Emery board. Miniature sewing kit. Scotch tape. Kleenex. Comb. Brush. Cassette. Herb tea. Lipsticks: peach, apricot, cinnamon, poppy-red.

"I adore the Village, don't you?" she asked me. "It's so alive!"

I smiled, trying to dazzle.

She yawned. "I'm wiped," she said. "I had a make-up call at six A.M. An early fitting with Anne Klein. And I was up late . . . seven bookings yesterday."

Yak, yak, yak. Skinny, skinny, skinny. I shot a look at YoYo who lowered her upper circle, eyes intent on antipasto.

"I'm so happy we're finally together!" Kimberley went on. She chatted with the waiter, calling him "Vinnie, darling!" as she ordered, "*Fettuccine Alfredo*, extra creamy!" Batting her eyelashes, she added, "*Zucchero. Mandorie di albicocche. Albume d'uova. Italia.*"

Vinnie darling! Show off! What a phony!

The waiter put down a basket of fresh rolls in front of her. Reaching for a hunk of bread, she dabbed lots of butter on the crust.

YoYo sighed as she finished her celery and pimiento.

I sighed as I finished my Caesar salad. We sighed together as we stared at Kimberley. Where did all the
calories go? I wondered, as I searched in vain for a
bulge under her yellow pants.

Kimberley picked a bread crumb off her lap as the
waiter served her pasta. "What are you doing this summer?" she asked us.

"Sunny California, same as always," YoYo replied.

Putting down her fork, Kimberley twisted a strand
of hair around her finger. "I'd like to be a mermaid on
a surfboard," she said in a dreamy kind of way.

"Then you wouldn't be able to wear pants," I said,
thinking that was pretty funny, but they both ignored
me.

"Why not fly out to California? We've just redecor-
ated the guest suite." YoYo was being generous, as usual.

"Thanks." After another bite, Kimberley said, "I *really*
wasn't looking for an invitation."

Not *really*, I thought, as I kicked YoYo under the
table.

Kimberley went on. "If only I could borrow your
palm trees and orange groves and tacos and — "

" — Smog? Earthquakes? Mud slides?" I couldn't help
being sarcastic. I wanted her hips instead of mine!

"And you, Maggie? What are *your* plans?" she replied
in a tone that suggested I'd have to make up a failed
course in summer school.

"We go to Martha's Vineyard. My parents rent a
cottage there." Suddenly, I saw myself in an album of
vacation snapshots. That's me bicycling to the post
office. There I am in front of the art gallery. Another
one of me buying live bait at the shack. I thought of

the boats returning late afternoon with lobster and sunfish. Almost everyone barefoot at the General Store. Waking in the misty dawn while others slept. The smell of the ocean as I sat on the grass eating grapes.

I wished I were there, at the Vineyard, instead of lunching at Giovanni's. I wished I were as beautiful as Kimberley. I wished for a brand-new me.

"I have a cousin whose parents own a house in Menemsha," Kimberley said.

But I was daydreaming. If only I could take my raft that very minute and go from beach to beach, Gay Head to Oak Bluff, swimming at the end of each day in the calm bay of Menemsha. If only my eyes were pale green. . . . "Menemsha?" I was startled.

"Yes," Kimberley said. "I often visit."

Had she been there recently? Did that explain her springtime tan?

"There are lots of wonderful guys at the Vineyard," she said.

I never met a wonderful guy there. I never met a wonderful guy anywhere.

She went on. "You're both so lucky, having all the fun, while I have to work." She opened her pocketbook and showed us her date book crammed with appointments. Then she asked me if I had a summer job. Without waiting for an answer, she said, "Thank heaven for Zach."

"Zach?" echoed YoYo, falling into the trap.

"You remember Zach?" Kimberley said to YoYo, who looked blank.

YoYo, I was sure, had never met a wonderful guy, either.

Kimberley continued. "Zach was going to be a lawyer, but with so many lawyers around, he's changed his mind." She put her date book back in her pocketbook. "Now, he can't decide between science and journalism."

YoYo nodded sympathetically, as if she, too, were going out with someone who had a similar problem.

"Or maybe he'll do something about the environment . . . the world's such a mess." Kimberley shrugged hopelessly.

YoYo shrugged hopelessly, also.

"I've been going with Zach ever since Sam and I broke up. You remember Sam?"

"The one after Jake?" YoYo looked like she had PMS cramps.

"Zach and I belong together." Kimberley spoke softly and then pulled away, as if she'd removed herself and gone somewhere else.

YoYo and I were quiet.

Kimberley surprised me by fixing her eyes right on mine and leaving them there. Why couldn't I look away? Was there something she wanted from me? But that was impossible. YoYo was wrong. We could never be friends. That was obvious from the beginning.

YoYo signed for lunch with her American Express card. "It's been great! Have a great summer!" She hugged us good-bye.

Kimberley said that she had to buy some wrinkle cream and would I like to come along? I couldn't figure her out. Did she honestly believe that I'd want to spend another minute with her? *Fettuccine Alfredo*, extra creamy! Blah blah *Italia*! Wrinkle cream! Who did she think she was? I told her that I was awfully sorry but I had to catch the three-fifty-seven back home to Port Washington. The "awfully sorry" part was a fib.

On the train, I stared out the window and kept seeing Kimberley. Why? I wondered. Not that I really cared.

Dear Maggie,

It was fun being together. Isn't Kimberley gorgeous? Whenever I'm with her I feel ugly and fat. I nearly flunked my Finals but didn't Thank God! Mom said no more hanging out at the pool this summer so I'm a Candy Striper in charge of milk shakes at the Hospitol. She said I should also stretch my mind so I'm taking a Great Books course for Enrichment which means not for credit just in case I fail. The Professor is cool and wears jeans and boots and a Cowboy Hat. We're reading Great Expectations which is boring. I hope I don't get jilted on my wedding day like poor Miss Havisham. I wonder if I'll ever have a wedding day. I bought a striped bikini but the stripes go the wrong way so I have to lose ten pounds by tomorrow. I'm fading away on selery and V-8 juice. Mommy and Daddy built a sauna near the pool so theres lots of company with everyone drinking champane. Last night Joan Collins was here with a wig. And Cher read fortunes with Tarot cards and said soon somebody would enter my life. You won't beleive this but right away Aunt Mabels son Roger called to invite me to The Grateful Dead consert. My father had his yearly checkup and they think they found something suspisious so he has to have a G.I. Series. I'm not sure what that is but they snap pictures of your insides. Give my love to your family and write real soon! Have a great time at Martha's Vineyard!

xxxx yoyo ☺

P.S.   Tomorrows my birthday and I'm praying my parents give me a horse.

P.P.S.   Excuse spelling!

# TWO

My father is a dentist. He's tall with silver sideburns. He wears a blue denim smock instead of a white one. He's so gentle that you hardly feel his rubber-gloved hands when they're in your mouth. His voice is low and sexy as he says, "Rinse please." Once he made a solid gold molar for my mother which she wears on a chain around her neck. He likes jazz and takes courses in Russian literature. He's read *Crime and Punishment* four times. "There's one thing in life you can't get enough of, Maggie, and that's education!" he tells me all the time.

My mother is an artist who doesn't like to be called that because she hasn't sold a painting yet. She teaches an adult education course called "Women Artists." She knows a lot about the paintings of Susan Rothenberg, Jennifer Bartlett, and Helen Frankenthaler. She's short with frizzy brown hair that she once had straightened but it didn't take. She reads all the latest books on psychology and adolescence. When we have an argument, she'll say, "It's okay to feel angry. You have every right." For some reason that I don't understand, that makes me furious.

I like watching her get ready to paint. Stretching the canvas, pouring the reds and yellows and blues into Campbell's soup cans, twirling the brushes. Her paintings are so large that she sometimes works on the floor. They look like brightly colored amoebas crawling in space. Over coffee, she'll ask me, "Is the orange too intense? Too much black?" as if she really cared what I thought. That makes me feel good.

My sister, Jenny, is . . . well, what shall I say? Everyone adores her. That's because she's pretty, too pretty. Straight dark bangs, wide-apart hazel eyes, and a handful of freckles dusted across her nose. She's seven, eight years younger than me. My mother had three miscarriages in between us and just when the doctor advised her to give up, she got pregnant again. This time she didn't lose the baby. She was ecstatic. My father was delighted. Relatives and friends told me I wouldn't be lonely anymore. Everyone makes assumptions when you're an only child:

1. You're spoiled.
2. You're a snob.
3. You're dying for a brother or sister.

All false, especially number 3. I loved having my own bathroom and my own shampoo.

Jenny follows me all the time. She bursts into tears

when I close my bedroom door. She doesn't understand that I need privacy. When I try to explain, she nods, but her eyes fill and her chin quivers off center. Then I feel guilty and make all sorts of promises. Parcheesi, Monopoly, a horror film, a carnival ride, fireworks at the beach. I end up polishing her nails hot-pink.

That's our family except for Eloise, our Miniature Schnauzer, who's going on fourteen, has epilepsy, and takes Dilantin.


It was raining when we arrived at the cottage on Martha's Vineyard. The first thing my mother did was to kick off her shoes. "It's so good to be back," she said. We all knew what she meant. My father brought in the bags. Jenny and I made up the beds. How we loved it here! Rocking chairs on either side of the fireplace. An open porch overlooking the meadow. A kitchen with geranium pots on the windowsill. Two bedrooms and a living room. A dormitory room upstairs with a view of an old weathered windmill.

One morning we were at the Center reading the bulletin announcing the events of the day. Square dance at 8:30. I thought of all the square dances I'd ever gone to hoping that Mr. Someone would be there waiting for me. He never was, so I spent most of my time hanging around the watercooler pretending to be thirsty. All I ever wanted was to be part of a pair. Spin your partner . . . dance to the right, and he'd be there. Mr. Someone who would phone while I was doing the dishes, whose french fries I'd share, who might try to kiss me under a chunk of moon.

"Maybe this time you'll be lucky," said Jenny, moving into my fantasy.

Then I noticed a pair of tanned legs, cutoff jeans, a man's button-down shirt, and a thick pigtail that swung around. She was surrounded by boys and girls, close as pearls on a string. Suddenly, I felt unwanted, as if I'd gone into the school cafeteria holding my tray, and all the tables were filled. I didn't want to see her. I didn't want her to see me.

Before I had a chance to break away, I heard a voice call out, "Maggie, hi! It's me, Kimberley! Remember?" She went on brightly, "This is Toby and Bimbo. Here's Munson, my cousin Clipper, and Snow." Then, saving him for last, "And this is Zach — Zach Powers." Cuddling against him, she nearly disappeared into his sweatshirt.

I introduced my parents and Jenny and hoped they'd leave right away. Then everyone smiled at everyone for a long time. Finally, my father grabbed Jenny's hand as my mother mumbled something about buying fish for dinner.

Tossing her hair, Kimberley said, "Zach and I couldn't bear another minute of Manhattan's heat wave so I phoned Clipper and . . ."

" . . . here we are," finished Zach.

I stared up at him. He was tall as a tree with red hair and a matching beard, and arms and legs like pick-up sticks. His hand crept into Kimberley's rear pocket and stayed there. I felt a funny tingle in the back of my knees as I imagined him kissing her.

How did they meet? I wondered. Dancing at a club?

Popcorn spilling onto one another at the movies? Rescuing kittens from the animal shelter? He was strong and virile, yet I could picture him reading poetry. KimberleyandZach. Their names ran together like finger paints.

"Going to the dance tonight?" Kimberley asked me.

Taken aback, I didn't know what to say. Perhaps, if I didn't answer, she might think I had another date, that I, too, was popular. I wasn't about to tell her how I longed for Mr. Someone, my Mr. Someone who never appeared.

"You should come," a voice said. Which one was he?

List of characters: Toby had acne; Bimbo's forefinger was very long; Clipper looked bleached next to Snow, who was black; KimberleyandZach; Munson, who was shorter than the others with chestnut curls.

"Well?" The voice had come from Munson. Exactly how tall was he? Perhaps, if I took off my shoes and danced barefoot . . . an inch or two . . . below the top of my head?

Spin your partner . . . dance to the left. I could almost hear the caller.

I said, "Okay." So much for romantic responses.


At home, I conditioned my hair with mayonnaise, creamed my face with Crisco, and cooled wet tea bags on my eyes. Then I lay on the floor and raised my legs so that the blood would rush to my head. I would glow! At least, that's what *Harper's Bazaar* said. I tried to slant my mind toward positive thinking. My mother once told me her mantra, so I borrowed it and meditated.

Then my mind drifted to the last fortune cookie whose message I'd saved:

> *Anticipate the good*
> *so that you may enjoy it.*

PLEASE, JUST THIS ONCE, LET IT BE WONDERFUL FOR ME!

Jenny barged in. "What's all this gook?"

"I'm trying to be beautiful."

"Like the girl at the Center? Kimberley? Who is she? A movie star? I'll bet *she* doesn't have to go through all that."

"No, she's lucky," I said.

"Aren't you jealous?"

"Don't be silly. What an awful way to go through life. Somebody's always going to have more than you."

"You sound like Mommy."

"Besides," I said, "you mean envious, not jealous."

"What's the difference?"

"Jealous means that you want something the other person has and you don't want her to have it. Envious means that you want what the other person has but you don't mind her having it." I was reciting something I'd read from a psychology book on my mother's night table.

"I don't get it," Jenny said.

"Envy is okay. Jealousy isn't," I explained.

"It's okay that Kimberley is really, *really* pretty and you're not?" Jenny always knew how to get straight to the point.

I glared at her. I was superstitious. If I kicked her

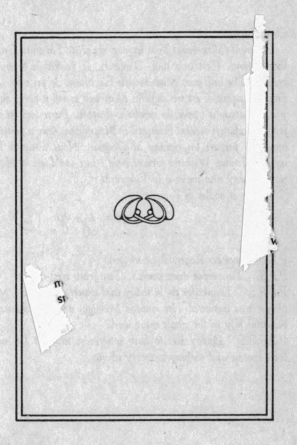

*Cher Maggie,*

*Comment t'allez-vous? Tous les jours are great! J'ai quitté Great Expectations. C'est trop dull. D'ailleurs, Je flunked le première examen. The hell avec Mademoiselle Havisham. Je prise le? la? Francais again. C'est très difficile. Mais well worth it parce qu'il y a un garçon a travers la vestibule. Il appelle Pierre and est un foreign exchange student Français. Et Magnifique! Avec a poitrine broad! Il prepare un examen de l'Anglais. Nous avons a lot instruire l'autre. Wish me fortune bien! I sure could use it. Have you met any new amies a la Vineyard?*

*Oodles et oodles de l'amour!*

xxxx yo yo ☺

P.S.    Remember Roger? Il est un geek!

P.P.S.    J'ai perdue deux pounds. C'est great! n'est-ce-pas?

P.P.P.S.    Thanks for the birthday card which got here late. My prayer was answered. Her name is Midnight and she's the most beautiful filly in the whole entire world.

P.P.P.P.S.    Daddy has to have some more tests but I'm sure there rootine and nothing to worry about.

# THREE

The next few days were hot and humid. I'd slip into a damp bathing suit and go down to the beach for a swim. Walking along the ocean's edge, I'd look for seashells and hold them against my ear listening for echoes.

One afternoon I saw Kimberley. She was all alone sitting on the sand near a child's pail and shovel. I didn't know whether or not to say hello. "Hi!" I blurted out, afraid she would turn away. But she smiled and waved. I went over and sat down next to her. She smelled of coconut oil.

We didn't say anything for a while and then she began to talk about herself. She was a model after school. I said that I helped in the attendance office. She was an only child. I had a younger sister. On weekend nights she dated. I didn't tell her that I baby-sat. She lived in New York City in an apartment opposite the Museum of Natural History. I said that I grew up in a white colonial house with blue wildflowers and a crab apple tree on the front lawn.

Staring at her, I thought that we were worlds apart. I'd never known anyone like her. My friends at home were different. Everything about them was predictable. We always did the same things. On Saturdays, we met in town for a cheeseburger. Then we went window-shopping; jeans and a top; leg warmers and jazz shoes; a Benetton sweater; an R.E.M. cassette. We usually ended up at the stationery store where we riffled through teen magazines. Then we'd go home and phone one another to make plans for the following Saturday. There was nothing to discover.

Everything about Kimberley fascinated me. Her profile as she gazed out at the ocean. The oiled slope of her shoulders. Her narrow hands with three antique rings on one finger. A waist the size of a bangle bracelet. The way she moved, like a ballerina. Even her voice. She said she was sixteen, but she seemed older, much older than me.

She had a habit of holding her hands together with her fingers raised in a little church steeple before she went off someplace, far away in her head. I wanted to follow. What are you thinking? Where are you? but something made me afraid she'd slip away if I asked too many questions. So, instead, I squeezed on some sunscreen and rolled over on my stomach.

"My father died when I was eleven," Kimberley said suddenly, looking up from the sand castle she was building. "His name was Theo."

I was shocked. I couldn't imagine life without a father. "How awful," I said. "Of what? Cancer?"

"An embolism."

"What's that?"

"A blood clot," Kimberly said. "He had a heart condition and lots of fat in his arteries. He was in the hospital for open-heart surgery when he keeled over and died. Just like that!" She snapped her fingers.

My mind painted a picture. Tubes and needles, a nurse running along the corridor, the PA system paging the surgeon, a cold body on the floor, a snapshot (wallet size) of Kimberley clutched inside the fist of her dead father.

She continued, "He had a family history of heart."

What was I doing thinking of valentines?

"His father had two heart attacks, his mother had angina, and his brothers suffered from hypertension." She rattled it off as if boasting.

"My grandmother died last year." It was all I could offer.

"Grandmothers are old. They're supposed to die," Kimberley said as she tied the straps of her bikini top.

I thought of show-and-tell in the early grades when no one seemed interested in what I shared.

"I was away at camp when Daddy died," she went on. "My mother phoned to say that the operation was a success but he was too weak to write to me."

"You mean he was dead the whole time?"

She nodded.

"Your mother lied to you?" I couldn't believe it.

"She told me on visiting day." Kicking the sand castle, she said, "We were taking a walk down to the lake. I remember there were pinecones on the path and . . ."

" . . . But what about the funeral?"

"My mother went without me. She thought coming home would ruin my summer." Kimberley stood and watched the waves roll in. Suddenly, she was no longer the most beautiful girl I'd ever seen. She was any young girl, wistful and yellow-haired, tripping over pebbles as she began sprinting down the beach.

I ran after her.

Kneeling on the wet sand, she started to dig furiously, faster and faster, until a clam rose up from the mud. "I'll never forgive my mother. *Never!*" she cried, as she wiped her hands on her gold-flecked legs. The clam tucked himself back into the sand.

We were quiet as the waves broke. Walking back to where we'd been sitting, Kimberley seemed sad.

I knew I should say something consoling, but I was too busy imagining the funeral. Figures in black, everyone sobbing, a sleeping Robert Redford in a coffin, the face of Kimberley's mother hidden by a veil, her body supported by relatives, each with their own frail hearts.

"Every Sunday we'd have cocoa at Rumplemeyer's . . ." I heard Kimberley say, " . . . at a table near the stuffed animals." She was sitting cross-legged on the sand, a tiny blue vein trickling down the inside of her thigh. "Daddy always wanted to know what I was doing, what I felt, was I happy?"

I was spellbound, a little girl hearing a story that she wanted to go on forever.

"He was born in Vienna and gave my mother twelve crystal wine goblets when they married. Blue, green, burgundy, turquoise, lavender, and amber." She gave a deep sigh. "Two of each."

It sounded so romantic. My parents were dull by comparison. There was nothing glamourous about my mother wearing a gold molar on a chain around her neck or my father saying, "Bite down, please."

"I thought it was a dream," Kimberley continued. "I waited for him to come home after work so that I could rush into his arms."

"Oh, Kimberley," was all I could say.

"In the beginning, I felt as if I'd done something wrong, as if I were being punished for being naughty." She dropped her voice so that I could hardly hear. "Does that sound crazy, Maggie?"

"Oh, no. I understand." I didn't. Not really. I tried to. She seemed to expect it.

Turning away, she sifted sand through her fingers. "Daddy was so handsome. Black wavy hair, dark eyes, and a pearl stickpin in his tie."

I blinked back tears. Something told me to be quiet.

"I kept hearing his voice. Even now, I try to make him come back but I can't."

I wanted to touch her, put my hand over hers. It was hard for me to do. I wasn't sure enough of myself. I didn't know if I had the right.

"Why am I telling you all this?" Kimberley got up. She had such a way of attracting attention that everyone stared at her as she ran toward the ocean. Waist-deep in waves, she called out, "Come on, Maggie!"

But I couldn't move. I was crying and didn't want her to see me. Did she share this with all her friends? Would she regret it and pretend that nothing important had been said? I was afraid of doing something wrong, afraid that, somehow, I'd disappoint her. Was it that day, or another, that I first began to worship her? Does it matter?

She came back, dripping water all over me. "You look sad, Maggie." She twisted her beach towel into a sarong. "Never feel sorry for me," she said. "*Never!* Besides, someday I'll inherit the wine goblets." Then, rubbing her sandy toes against mine, she said, "I like being with you. I don't have to pretend to be someone else."

I felt some hidden promise, something unsaid.

"Maggie? What are you thinking? Where are you?"

How could I tell her my fantasy? That, more than anything in the world, I wanted to be like her. To look like her, talk like her, walk like her, think like her. Even more, I wanted to become her. She was perfect! She knew about life. She knew about death. She had suffered.

How I envied her.

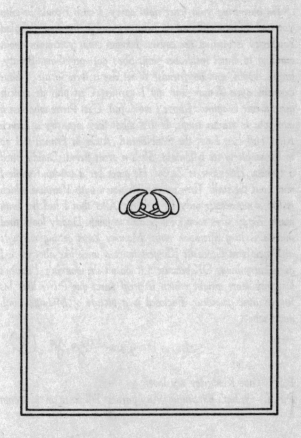

*Dear Maggie,*

*I'm answering your letter right away. I wish I could be with you and the windmill and the fishermen and go barefoot. I'm glad Kimberley is visiting her cousin. I know what you mean about wanting to crawl inside her skin. She's got everything! Beauty, brains, boobs, and boyfriends! What else is there in life? I have examens apres-demain and am I terrifier! C'est plus de difficile que I'd ever imagined. I hope I won't fail. C'est Pierre who kissed moi pour le premier temps. Is that what they mean by a French Kiss? Ha! Ha! I got the tremblements. Apres la Francaise I go to the stable to see Midnight. She's a great freind! Daddy hired a trainer. His name is Ziggy. He gives her a workout while I muck out the stall. Then we rub her down with Vetroline which is like a moisterizer only for a horse. After that I feed her bran mash. Ziggy says soon we'll be able to jump! Daddy looks tired and takes long afternoon naps. Mommy keeps getting messages and facials at Georgette Klingers twice a week like always so I guess everythings OK because if it wasn't she wouldn't. I haven't lost any more weight which is great parce-que Pierre likes his femmes avec grandeur. Enclosed is a picture of Midnight with guess who?*

xxxx yo yo ☺

*P.S.    Give Kimberley my love!*

*P.P.S.    What's happening? Any parties? Fill me in on the scoop!*

# FOUR

Jenny, as usual, followed me from the bedroom to the bathroom and back to the bedroom. I'd changed tops five times. Nothing looked right. Not even the jeans. It was a fat day.

"I'm mad at you," she said. "We don't do anything together anymore. And you've changed. You're different." She made a face.

"We do too," I said. "Last week we read Judy Blume books every day." Grumpy. "*How* am I different?"

"I'm not sure, but I like you better the other way." She trotted after me down the steps, through the living room, to the porch where my mother and father were having vodka and tonics.

"We never see you these days," remarked my mother. "Where to now?" After a moment, "Kimberley?"

"Out," I said.

"Out?" repeated my father. He was annoyed. I could

tell by his mouth. His lips narrowed into a mailbox slot when he was angry.

"A clambake," I explained.

"Why don't we have a clambake *here* sometime?" he asked.

I got the message: You're never home. We see less and less of you. We don't know your new friends. We used to spend more time being a family.

What about me? There were things that bothered me also. I'm the only one who has a curfew. It shows lack of trust, I might have complained. Nonsense! they'd reply, their voices pasted together. Setting limits means that we care.

Then I'd continue with . . .

And they'd explain that . . .

What was the use? They'd never see it my way. Besides, I was already ten minutes late. "See you later." I ran down the path.

"That's exactly what I mean," I heard Jenny say.

Was it true? Had I changed? But wasn't that part of growing up? I still did my chores. I scoured the bathtub ring and made my bed and Jenny's when she forgot. I wiped grease from the stove and walked to the post office for the mail. Did they expect me to share everything in my life with them? What was the point of reading all those books on adolescence? Did they want me to be independent or not?

Why was I feeling so guilty?

At the beach, Snow had dug a sand pit about a foot deep. Clipper and Toby were gathering rocks. Zach and Munson stretched a huge tarp. Bimbo was building a fire.

"You're in charge of the corn, Maggie," directed Zach. "Husk the ears, but leave on the last couple of layers to cover the food later." He showed me how.

I loved to look at Zach. His beard, crayon-red. Tufts of hair, soft as yarn, poked out of the open collar of his polo shirt. He was hard and lean. Did he work out? Or was he lucky enough to inherit great muscle genes? He was so sure of himself. Not like a teenager at all. Why did I feel shy whenever he was near?

Munson was washing wet-rock seaweed in a pail of water. "Emeralds for you," he said, offering me a bunch.

"Yuk!"

"Turning me down?"

"I have a date with a crab."

Our conversation went like that. A volleyball over a net. You serve. I return. It was always a game.

Kimberley crouched in the sand, her legs folded under her. She and Zach were scrubbing small lobsters. He whispered something in her ear. She blushed.

If only Munson would whisper something in *my* ear! Then I could blush like Kimberley. "Listen . . ." I began.

He raised his head. "Crab stand you up?"

It's hopeless, I thought, and said, "No, he just phoned from the florist for my address." I tried to be clever in the same way they all seemed to be. If I copied them, then maybe they'd like me as much as Kimberley.

Bimbo was strumming the guitar with his long fingernail as he sang to Toby.

"I can feel the love inside my own,
Touch your need inside me.
Remember words that made you moan,
Vows I gave thee."

Then he told us the lyrics were his own.

"It's a lonely song," Kimberley said.

What made her see it that way? I wondered, as I watched everyone become a pair. Munson plopped my hand in the pail. Clipper and Snow wiped chickens for broiling. Toby and Bimbo cleaned sweet potatoes. Kimberley and Zach split franks.

The sun had set. I felt that I belonged. All of us together. I held the moment. Studying each one, I quickly placed a detail in my mind to remember and return to. Snow who was the color of freshly brewed coffee, Clipper, pale as a vanilla milk shake. A blemish on Toby's chin. Bimbo's long fingernail. Munson's ringlets misted by salt air. Kimberley, a yellow ribbon tied to Zach, skinny as a spider.

Munson took my hand out of the bucket and brushed it against his lips. Later, I'd think of it as a kiss. My first kiss.

Bimbo and Snow lined the pit, placing chicken wire over it. We all put down a layer of hard-shelled clams. Afterward, Zach and I covered the food with corn husks, then he poured a bucket of sea water on the top. Finally, the wet tarp.

"It won't be ready for an hour," Bimbo said, opening bottles of Coke.

We spread blankets on the sand and stared out at

the ocean. Someone played tapes and we all sang, with Bimbo doing harmony.

"Okay," Snow broke in. "We're called for an audition and we have to cut a record. The producer says we're hot. Let's go for a gold! We need a name. Something catchy!"

"The Crabs," suggested Munson.

We all laughed.

"Come on, the pressure's intense," said Snow. "The producer's breathing down my back. I've got a percentage deal hanging. A little pizzazz, please."

"The Surfers," said Clipper.

Snow didn't like it. "Too foamy."

"The Jelly Fish," from Toby.

"Slimy." Snow shuddered. "Something with a beat, in sync with the times."

Zach sounded impatient as he said, "Who cares?"

"Not bad," remarked Snow. "I like it. Possibilities, The Who Cares. There's a native quality, primitive, raw." He tapped his foot and swayed from side to side. "De dum de dum de dum." He began to dance. "The Who Cares." Snow grinned.

Meanwhile, the bake continued to steam.

Someone pointed out the Big Dipper. Then the North Star. After that, Neptune, Pluto, Mars, Jupiter.

"The pendant world," Kimberley said softly.

"Shakespeare!" Bimbo cried out.

"How did you know that?" I was impressed.

"It's a game of quotes," he replied with a shrug. "Kimberley made it up. Whenever I'm not sure, I just guess Shakespeare."

"Here's one," said Zach, looking up at the dark sky. "The forget-me-nots of the angels."

"Shakespeare," I said, wanting to play, thinking this was the way.

He shook his head. "Longfellow."

Disappointed, I stuck out my tongue at Bimbo.

"World without end," Kimberley said.

"The Bible." Zach identified it right away.

Everyone around me was so smart. Were they all some kind of geniuses? A clique of kids with incredibly high potential? Kimberley and Zach each went to private schools where, I imagined, class members lounged on contour chairs and passed around pizza as they quizzed one another on Shakespeare. And the others probably carried around *Bartlett's* and a thesaurus racking their brains to find the best quote.

I heard Zach continue, "How do I love thee? Let me count the ways. I love thee to the depth and breadth and height — "

Kimberley broke in, "A place to stand and love in for a day. With darkness and the death-hour rounding it."

Elizabeth Barrett Browning. Even *I* knew that. But no one said a word. We watched Kimberley and Zach who were so close that they could have been the poet and her lover, Robert. Except that Kimberley wasn't an invalid.

"These blessed candles of the night," Munson recited.

"Shakespeare." This time I had to be right.

"Bravo!" he shouted, before going over to lift the tarp at one corner. "It's puffing up," he called out to the others.

Bimbo peered inside to make sure the clams had opened. Clipper melted the butter as Zach passed paper towels.

"This is better than McDonald's!" kidded Snow, an ear of corn in one hand and a lobster claw in the other.

I noticed Kimberley opening a bottle of wine. Where had it come from? I'd seen only soft drinks around earlier. She handled the corkscrew with ease, removing the cork as expertly as my father extracting a tooth. Then she poured some into a dixie cup and passed it. I didn't know what to do. My parents permitted wine on birthdays, Thanksgiving, Christmas, and after someone died. Be cool. I told myself. Kimberley giggled as she made a toast, "To The Who Cares!" Everyone took a sip, including me. I suppose I could have spilled mine onto the sand, but I didn't. I just drank it and tried to look sophisticated.

What's the big deal? I always made too much of everything. I wanted to be liked, to be part of their world. Nothing was more important to me at that time. I felt the beginning of a wheeze. I pretended it was a cough, nothing more, and concentrated on deep breathing. Kimberley stared at me for a moment, her eyes pushing into mine. I was overwhelmed, afraid that I might not be able to handle it. I wasn't even sure what "it" was. Everything was getting to be too much. Even Kimberley. Maybe I should have stayed home with my parents and Jenny, after all.

"Is it my imagination or does the Big Dipper look dippy?" asked Zach.

Suddenly, there was a strange yet familiar smell. Where was I? Outside the school cafeteria? The gym?

No, I was sitting on a blanket on the sand and Clipper was rolling a joint. I panicked. Now what? It went from Clipper to Snow, who took a drag. Then Bimbo. Then to Toby who inhaled slightly and passed it to me. I quickly shoved it toward Munson, who didn't dare. Then Zach, who did. Finally, Kimberley who flicked it into the black night and shrugged as if bored.

I didn't understand her, or else I wasn't ready for her. But I wanted to be. I needed to be. I had this feeling that she was saying something to me. If only I knew what it was.

"Care for a piece of planet?" asked Bimbo to no one in particular.

"I'm stuffed, ate too much already," joked Toby.

Kimberley and Zach moved toward one another. Cupping her face in his palms, he kissed her, a long movie-kind of kiss. Then one of his hands dropped somewhere below her shoulders.

I looked down at my breasts.

"Skinny dipping, anyone?" Bimbo began taking off his QUÉ PASA T-shirt.

I heard a raspy hoarseness deep inside my chest. Oh, no! I'd forgotten my allergy pills! My parents would be furious. What if my throat closed and I stopped breathing? What if my mother and father had to claim my dead body on the beach? What if they saw the wine? Smelled pot? I shut my eyes, terrified of my wheeze, even more terrified of bare bottoms bobbing up and down in the surf.

Then, miraculously, Kimberley's voice. "Make a wish! A falling star!" distracting everyone. "The mosquitoes are killing me! Had enough, Maggie?"

I shot her a grateful look and followed her past the deserted shack, the rocks of the jetty, past the lifeguard stand and the boathouse. I stumbled after her until we reached the road. Once there, I could breathe again. I would have followed her further. Anywhere! She'd rescued me. I promised myself that one day I would repay her.

No matter what.

*Dear Maggie,*

*I'm waiting for my final French grade but I'm sure I flunked. The professor said to study for a multiple choice test then he gave us an essay which isn't fair! Pierre went back to Paris because his parents are getting a divorce. So I'm sans boy freind which is nothing new n'est-ce pas? I don't feel to bad because I helped him avec l'anglais and he taught me how to kiss. I wish he'd write. Maybe it's to soon. I'm still on a diet but haven't lost anymore and I'm not eating anything! My mother made an appointment with an akupuncturist for what's called weight reduction. Daddy has to go to Cedars Hospitol for more tests. When I ask him how he's feeling he pats me on the head and cracks a joke. He's never hungry and his pants are baggy. Mommy is taking cooking lessons from Dinah Shore. She taught our Mexican couple how to make jambalaya which you'd love except your allergic to shrimp and oysters. There anniversary is tomorrow and Daddy gave her a bracelet watch with 350 tiny little diamonds. She's giving him a silver Mercedes to match hers. I'm spending more and more time with Midnight. She loves it when I put on her bridle and saddle. She's getting to be my best freind. Sometimes I'm lonely. I wish I was with you and Kimberley. I miss Pierre. It was great having someone finally! Lately I've been sleeping at the stable. Ziggy comes early in the morning with cocoa and blueberry muffins so the three of us eat together.*

xxxx yo yo ☺

*P.S. I'm sorry about your wheezes.*
*P.P.S. What do you and Kimberley talk about?*

# *FIVE*

*I* woke up the next morning with still another wheeze. I always had allergies to certain things. Nuts, chocolate, shrimp, caviar, which I threw up one New Year's Eve, cat hair, dog hair, but only if it shed like a golden retriever's, mold, dust, February snow, May pollen, wool — the itchy kind — and certain pillows if they weren't hypoallergenic.

It happened when I was born. I came out of my mother bunting-pink and soon turned red and raw with a whistle in my chest. My parents, I'm told, nearly climbed into my crib to be sure I was breathing while the vaporizer steamed away wallpaper lions and tigers and elephants.

Everyone said it was psychological, due to stress. How ridiculous! As if I were a tense embryo biting my nails in the womb. My allergies were hereditary. I was certain of it even if there was no proof.

Rain splashed against my window. It was going to

be an awful day. Benadryl or tedryl every four hours and a metahaler twice a day. I'd get the shakes and be spacey. Not that it mattered, not that anything mattered since last night. I could hear them, my new ex-friends. "Oh, her . . ." they'd already dismissed me. "Just a kid with a wheeze."

I went downstairs. Jenny was sulky because her friend on the other side of the windmill had a double-ear infection and couldn't come out to play. My mother was finishing a collage. She was a slob and used her art as an excuse to avoid housework. My father was re-reading *War and Peace* as a tape of Gerry Mulligan and his saxophone played in the background. Eloise — ears flattened — barked and hid behind the toilet because she was afraid of the rain.

I collapsed on the couch. Instead of the usual, What's the matter? Feel like talking? there was silence. I could always tell when my parents were reading the latest on teenage development. They went overboard on privacy. Less questions, no prying. I groaned in a melodramatic way. Didn't they care how miserable I was? Didn't they want to know what happened? I needed someone to say, I love you.

I'd behaved like a geek. Now, everybody would have a great time without me. Everybody would go sailing. Everybody would play miniature golf. Everybody would stroll, hand in hand, from one party to the next. Everybody would walk on prickly weeds to buy turquoise bracelets from the Native Americans in their souvenir stands.

"Everybody! Who are these everybodies?" my father often demanded. "There are always going to be everybodies, Maggie. I suggest you stop comparing yourself to others." Thin lips, mailbox slot, as he continued, "Do you intend to go around feeling sorry for yourself whenever things don't go your way?" Why, I wondered, did he always make me feel better even when he scolded?

Tossing around on the couch, I saw my mother and father exchange glances. Interfere or not? They were like a pair of matching lamps, their heads like two clear globes through which I read their minds. Stay out of it, they agreed silently. He flipped another page of his book. She snipped a piece of ruffle from an old curtain. Then my father surprised me by coming over to kiss me. My mother handed me a swatch of fabric that she'd cut into a huge heart.

"Why can't everyone leave me alone?" I burst into tears and ran to my room.

I'd just finished washing my hair when I heard the doorbell. Then, Kimberley's voice. What would she think? Everything was a mess! The coffee table was covered with a squeezed tube of Nivea, cherry pits staining paper napkins, torn paperbacks, medical journals, art magazines. On the floor were mayonnaise bottles of acrylic paints, pillows from the couch, a can of Tab, and sand that hadn't been swept. And everywhere, the smell of wet bathing suits and stinky sneakers.

With my hair still sopping wet, I ran downstairs. Kimberley was already in the living room. I was horrified to see my mother, rear end up, still sprawled over old greeting cards, rags, and shellac. My father was labeling tapes. "Hi!" they greeted her warmly, a bit too casually, I thought. If the president of the United States stopped by, they'd continue with what they were doing and wave to some leftover coffee and cake. Jenny, at least, gave Kimberley the attention she deserved, even if she only stared.

Dragging Kimberley into my bedroom, I shut the door. Message: Jenny, keep out! Then we talked.

"About last night," I began. "When Bimbo — "

She broke in, "Nothing would have happened. Bimbo's terrified of the ocean. He doesn't even know how to swim."

"Honestly?"

"You're so naive, Maggie. Don't you see?"

I didn't know then what she meant. It would take me a long time before I understood. I had no reply. I sat silent and let the subject drop. Then, "What's it like to be a model?" I asked.

"It's fun when I get to keep the clothes. But boring, mostly. The money's fantastic. My mother says I need it for college. Sometimes I get tired and wish I could turn down an assignment. Today it's modeling. After that . . ." She didn't finish.

"Do you believe in God?"

"Nope," as if it didn't matter whether she did or not. "Do you?"

"Yes, I'd be afraid not to." Something I'd never admitted to anyone before.

"Why?" She studied the titles in my bookshelf.

"He might punish me."

"He? Have you ever thought that maybe God's a she?" Holding *Wuthering Heights* so gently that it might have been a wounded animal, she exclaimed, "I adored this!" Her gaze touched upon me for a moment. "Why would anyone want to punish *you*?"

I wasn't about to say. What kind of response did she expect? From the very first, when she asked a question, I felt she sometimes challenged me. Confused, I didn't know how to answer and said instead, "It's my favorite book. I brought it from home." And then, "I'm positive God's a he!"

"Like Santa?" She put the book back. "With apple cheeks and a white beard?" Turning to face me, she said, "Do you think God has nothing better to do than concentrate on you?"

"Too risky. I can't take that chance."

"Superstitious?"

I nodded. "Very!"

Kimberley ran a palm over her hair, dipped her eyelashes, and said playfully, "Let's hire a private jet and fly to California."

"We'll have tacos and enchiladas with YoYo," I replied, going along.

"And a sauna afterward."

"She'll introduce us to movie stars."

"Maggie and Kimberley, this is Luke Perry." Kimberley pretended to be YoYo.

We burst out laughing.

Then, out of the blue, she said, "My mother takes Valium."

"How come?"

"She's always taken Valium. That and other tranquilizers, for as long as I can remember."

"Is she old?" I pictured Kimberley with gray hair.

"Mmmmm, forty-four."

"Does she work?"

"Of course! She says she has to so that I can stay in private school. The tuition's a fortune. I couldn't care less but that's what *she* wants." Kimberley smiled with her mouth but not with her eyes. "My mother loves being a martyr."

Yanking my pillow from the bed, I put it on the floor for Kimberley. She put her head on it and kicked off her sneakers. Even her bare toes were pretty, I noticed as I sat next to her. Not like mine, which were crooked and overlapped. "What does she do?" I asked.

"Manages a boutique on Madison Avenue. Designer clothes, the ones with one name like Adolfo, Chanel, Halston."

"Is she pretty?"

"Angela's in a relationship with Dr. Multz. He's a plastic surgeon, tits, ass, thighs, jowls, he lifts everything." She gave it some thought. "Yes, I suppose Angela's pretty."

Angela. I saw an angel with wings. Imagine a mother with wings! I thought of my own with a paint smear on her chin. Angela. Was that how Kimberley *always* referred to her?

"Multz is crazy about Charlie Chaplin. He insists I come along when they see his old films." Kimberley got up to imitate the comedian, his funny walk with turned-out flat feet, using an invisible cane and a make-believe hat. "Multz sees himself as my stepfather." She stopped, suddenly looking weary. "As if that were possible, as if anyone could . . ." Her voice was dull and sleepy. She seemed to slip away just as we were having fun. Then, abruptly, her mood changed as she teased,

"Wouldn't you love to sleep with Baryshnikov?"

The dancer? I wondered what it was like to sleep with anybody except Eloise whose wet black nose was often on my pillow at night.

She began to dance, showing me each step. "First position, second position, third, *pas de deux*." Did she have any idea how lovely she was to watch? "*Entre-chat.* I'm reading about Sylvia Plath. *Tour j'eté.* Have you read any of her poetry? You must! She was so scared. *Plié.*"

As we talked we discovered things in common:

1. We hated yogurt — even with raspberries.
2. Deodorant soap gave us a rash.
3. We saved scent strips from magazines.
4. Jade was our favorite gemstone.
5. Bambi made us cry.

"What's it like having a sister?" Kimberley asked.

"A pain! What's it like living in New York City?"

"The galleries are romantic. I love the smell of roasting chestnuts." She made everything so vivid. I saw myself standing in line for the latest exhibit. I could almost smell the smoky chestnuts.

Then I heard her say, "I make straight A's in school." Sometimes she skipped around. It was like playing hopscotch, jumping from box to box.

"You're a brainiac!" I said.

"It's important to my mother," Kimberley explained. "Sometimes I study so hard I don't know when to stop. I've had lessons in everything. Piano, art, dance, voice, tennis. It's important to be the best." She moved closer to me and suggested blow-drying my hair. She sang above the whine of the dryer. I was shocked at the richness of her voice, the way it parted from the rest of her. It wasn't at all fragile or delicate. Something about a blackbird. Bye, bye, blackbird. I'd never heard it before, nor since.

She told me that she was terrified of elevators, that she had difficulty walking by tall buildings. She couldn't leave the photographer's studio and hail a taxi unless there was a doorman nearby. Afterwards, she made fun of her fears, their silliness.

What else did we talk about?

Nearly *everything*.

"I'm lonely on Sundays." Hers.

"If you had one wish, what would it be?" Mine.

"For Daddy to be alive. And you?" Hers, of course.

"A boyfriend. My very own boyfriend." Mine, this time.

She remembered that she cried the first day of kindergarten. I couldn't find my cubby. Miss Lavell was her first grade teacher. Miss Castelluccio was mine. She learned to read before the others. I began biting my nails. She once stole a lipstick from the five and ten. I threw a dart at Jenny's ankle and made her promise not to tell. Then we discussed clothes and school and boys — ordinary things.

If only this day could go on and on! I'd never felt so close to a friend before. "Are you in love with Zach?" I asked.

"Yes," she said softly.

In love, on love, under love, what did it feel like? Multiple choice quiz. Check one.

a) I feel safe.
b) I feel important.
c) I feel tingly.

What about sex? I longed to ask. Maybe she'd get angry. She had every right. I wanted to know what she said, what she did. I wanted to hear the very words she used when she and Zach made love.

"Tell me about your house in Port Washington," Kimberley said.

I was disappointed. I wished for details about Zach. "I've lived there since I was born." Then I told her how the white paint on the outside always peeled and the black shutters needed new hinges. I described the blue wildflowers and the crab apple tree on the front lawn. The flagstone path through which four-leaf clovers have sprung and the brook that ran along the back, down where the pachysandra ends. You walk into a large hallway with a toy chest for boots. To the left, a sunny living room, a fireplace, and lots of windows with white curtains. To the right, a dining room with its collection of pewter. Then the kitchen with linoleum that's worn out where the dishwasher leaked. A radiator pipe warms the tiny powder room downstairs. A staircase leads to three bedrooms upstairs.

Cutting in, Kimberley said, "I love old houses!" her expression somewhat dreamy, as if imagining nooks and crannies, a musty attic filled with ice skates, Girl Scout badges, a baton, a lumpy Raggedy Ann doll with one leg missing.

I went on about the spool bed in my room and the connecting door to Jenny's bedroom, which has wallpaper scalloped like icing on a birthday cake. A crocheted spread covers my parents' double bed. Jazz records, books, and smelly turpentine rags are everywhere.

"Your wheeze is gone," Kimberley remarked.

I paused to take a deep breath. She was right. I hadn't even noticed.

Suddenly, a boom of thunder. Eloise whimpered and scratched at the door. I opened it and Kimberley bent down to pick her up. Cradling Eloise in her arms, she kissed her ears and nose and whiskers. Soft as a lullabye, she crooned, "Don't be scared, please don't be scared." Moving one hand along Eloise's warm belly, Kimberley felt the heartbeat before announcing, "Eloise is having an anxiety attack!"

Eloise had pulled her tail between her legs. Shivering with fright, she listened to the rain that fell in stripes against the window. "Think of something happy," Kimberley said. "A bone? Kibble? A long walk? A brushing?" Then she put Eloise back on the floor. Playful, teasing, Kimberley began racing around the room. Crouching in back of the rocking chair, she peeked through the wooden slats and cried out, "Boo!"

Eloise pricked up her ears.

"Boo!" called out Kimberley from inside the closet.

Eloise cocked her head.

"Boo!" Kimberley had crawled, half-hidden, under my bed.

Sniffing, sniffing, Eloise trotted across the floor and wriggled beside Kimberley. Tail thumping beneath the bed frame, she licked Kimberley's face and barked back, "Boo!"

Kimberley and I got the giggles. Eloise was smiling, also.

Squirming out from under the bed, Kimberley came up with the idea that we share a secret. "Something you've never told anyone," she said, brushing blanket fuzz from her jeans.

"You first." Was it a game? I wondered.

"No, you!" she insisted.

Should I tell her about my scary dream? The one I knew by heart? There is a house. I'm in the cellar. It's dark and dirty. There is a door and a window but just the same I can't get out. I'm trapped. I feel as if I'm being punished and I don't know why. No, I can't tell that to anyone. Not even Kimberley. "Well," I said instead, "I didn't vote for a friend of mine when she ran for class secretary."

"Why not?" Kimberley was lying on the floor again, gazing up at the ceiling.

"She was too snooty." I sprawled out next to her.

"Did you tell her that you did?"

"I never said that I didn't."

"Was she elected?"

"No."

Kimberley sat up and squinted at me. "Did you feel awful?"

I sat up, too. "Not particularly."

We giggled.

"Now, what's *your* secret?" I asked.

She began right away. "Once upon a time there was a handsome man and his wife and a little girl called — "

I had to break in. "Kimberley?"

"She went walking with her father every Sunday afternoon." Kimberley turned away before I could see her tears.

I didn't want her to cry then, not when the story was getting good, so I pretended not to notice. "Were they rich?" I asked.

"Yes, they lived in an apartment with a terrace." Twisting a strand of hair around her finger, she described parties with waitresses in frilly aprons. "And then . . ." she stopped.

I couldn't wait. "And then what?" I asked impatiently.

"They stopped being rich. But they still adored one another, whispering and touching all the time." Kimberley gave a deep sigh. "They always smelled good."

I, too, gave a deep sigh.

"One day," she continued, "the little girl saw her mother pulling out a suitcase from the closet. When the little girl asked where she was going, her mother said she had to visit a relative who was sick. That night the little girl heard her parents fighting. Her mother said that she was leaving and her father kept saying, "No, please . . . no please."

Was Kimberley telling me things she never told another person?

"Nothing happened," she said, narrowing her eyes. "The suitcase was gone the next morning and the handsome man died a few years later. The mother and child moved to a tiny apartment." With a shrug of her thin shoulders, she added, "No more terrace." Kimberley stood up and roamed around a bit, stopping in front of my dresser. "May I?" she asked, picking up an atomizer and spraying toilet water on her ankles.

"But what's the secret?" I wanted to know, thinking that I'd never seen anyone put cologne on their ankles before.

Surprised that I hadn't understood, she said, "That it wasn't what it seemed, saying one thing, doing another. They never knew I overheard their fight, which was *my* secret." She paused, but only for a minute. "Now," she said in a dramatic way, "the secret is *yours*, too."

It was getting too deep for me. "Maybe you have it all wrong," I said. "Couldn't it have been a misunderstanding?"

But Kimberley never even heard me. She was leaning on the windowsill, staring out at the windmill. "Angela still mourns Daddy, puts a phony, sad look on her face for their wedding anniversary and holidays."

"Maybe she really misses him." I thought Kimberley was being a little unfair.

"With Dr. Multz hanging around?"

I could think of nothing to say.

Kimberley reached for her bag and took out a silver pillbox. It was oval-shaped and dented. She flipped it open. Orange, yellow, red, green, blue, pink, turquoise — I had never seen so many pills! Then she pulled out a brown bottle. The four-ounce kind used for cough syrup. She twisted the cap off and gulped down two yellow capsules. "A few a day with apple juice keep the migraines away." She snapped the lid of the pillbox and closed the bottle. "Don't worry, Maggie," she said coldly. Her voice was distant, as if she were suddenly far away, out of my reach. *Snap*. Part of her was inside the pill box. *Snap. Snap.*

DON'T SHUT ME OUT! WHAT ARE THOSE HEAD-ACHES? ARE YOU SICK OR WHAT? SHARE THEM WITH ME! I WANT TO FEEL THEM JUST LIKE YOU. DON'T LEAVE ME!

"Anyone for cocoa?" my mother called from downstairs.

Kimberley's expression brightened. "I love cocoa on a rainy day!" She sounded happy, too happy. Her swift mood changes never failed to amaze me. I couldn't have known it then, but I'd soon grow to expect them.

Eloise scurried down the steps after us. In the living room, Jenny was playing checkers with my father. The collage was on the floor with a large needle and a spool of thread, wet clumps of Kleenex, and a bottle of glue. Paintings were propped against the wall.

Kimberley was on her second cup of cocoa when she said to my mother, "I wonder . . . would you care to do a painting of me?"

I couldn't believe what I'd heard. Why would Kimberley suggest such a thing? It didn't sound like her at all. I was positive my mother would refuse. She never did portraits. She dripped abstracts. Kimberley could hardly be a blob.

My mother glanced at me before replying, "Yes, I'd like that very much." Then, doing something funny with her tone, she added, "When?"

"Sometime." Kimberley was vague. "Sometime soon."

I watched her leave, skipping along the path and

leaping over puddles, raindrops sliding down her yellow slicker.

"What gleaming teeth!" my father said. "Comes from daily flossing."

I couldn't wait to run upstairs to spray toilet water on my ankles. But there was one thing I couldn't figure out. I knew that my mother hadn't been completely won over by Kimberley. But I couldn't bring myself to ask why.

*Dear Maggie,*

  *I can't get you out of my mind. Do you beleive in E.S.P.? We must be connected in some way. I keep thinking of you. Maybe its because Kimberley wrote me and said she likes you. She said your so natural. Don't tell her I told you. She hardly ever writes. Something is happening with me and Ziggy only I can't explain it. He was teaching me to jump and when I got off Midnight my spur got caught and I fell into his arms and he kissed me. The thing is I never thought of Ziggy that way. He's not tall or handsome or cool. The problem is that I liked it and before I knew what I was doing he kissed me again and I wanted to. What I don't know is how can you feel something you had no idea you felt to begin with? I'm so mixed up. When I go to bed at night I see him and remember the smell of hay and manure and I can't sleep. Afterward we sat near the fence where Midnight and me jump. We held hands and talked about his childhood which was mizerable and I told him about Daddy and some other things I've never told anyone not even you. I've never felt this way before. Pierre was different. I'm not sure why. Maybe it was the Kulture. I guess I'd feel better if I wasn't all alone with these strange feelings. I have no one to talk to. I can't tell Kimberley I'd feel silly. Do <u>you</u> ever feel these feelings? Write back real fast and tell me if you do.*

*xxxx yoyo* ☺

*P.S.   I got a 65 on the French test which is so so but the experience was great!*

*P.P.S.   Whose Munson?*

# SIX

*I*t was a lazy time. There was nothing I had to do. No school. No homework. No allergist appointment. One night I couldn't sleep so I tiptoed to the kitchen for a slice of watermelon and sat outside spitting pits on the dew-drenched grass. Sometimes . . . a stroll down to the dock to see the boats . . . lying on my raft in Menemsha's pond . . . a game of jacks with Jenny . . . an early evening movie at the Center with The Who Cares . . . moments at the beach with Kimberley . . . talking . . . just talking. One day I bumped into her with Zach at the fruit stand. I watched as their hands kept touching over the cherries and plums. Would I join them? they'd asked, unable to take their eyes off one another. I said no and bought a basket of blueberries before going home.

Morning sounds. The birds outside my window called me. My mother was rattling around in the living room. The screen door slammed. My father had gone

for the paper. Jenny was jumping rope on the porch.
Eloise growled at the tomato plants in the vegetable
garden.

I buried my head into my pillow. Maybe I'd lie in
the hammock and read all day. I could pretend I was
a little girl again . . . a castle, a prince, and me. Or, I
could pretend I was on *Oprah*, a finalist in a "Teenagers
Speak Out" contest.

Summer daydreams.

I heard the phone ring.

"Maggie," my mother called. "It's for you."

I ran downstairs in my nightgown. "Hello?"

"Hi! It's me, Munson. How 'bout tonight? Okay?"
His words sounded like a telex.

"Intense!" I telexed back, wondering how he'd gotten
my phone number. He must have asked Kimberley.

"Just you and me, kiddo."

"What about the others?"

"What others?"

Was he talking about a real date? Without Kimberley
and Zach? Without The Who Cares? Where would we
go? What would we talk about? The very idea terrified
me. If only there was a rock concert in Edgartown!
Bruce Springsteen had been there the week before.
Headlines in the Gazette . . . a mob scene, rock mania,
crushed bodies, jagged-edged bottles, pot, an ambu-
lance. . . . I'd devoured the details. Springsteen. All
right! Dance in the aisles, join in the encore. We want
more! We want more! I'd concentrate on the spotlight
and stop worrying about what to say or how to behave.
The cheers of the crowd would take care of everything.

A plea from the management to quiet down. Everyone spaced out in the parking lot.

Munson kept talking. "We'll walk the drag, grab a pizza. There are a million things . . ."

". . . A movie?" That seemed safe.

"What I'd really like . . ." He paused for a moment over the phone.

"Yes?"

". . . is to watch a sunset."

"A what?"

"A sunset. You know, sun . . . go . . . down. A peak experience, Maggie. Loosen up, kiddo. I'll even polish my moped for you," he'd laughed into the receiver before hanging up.

So, there we were, hours later, perched on the cliffs at Gay Head. A threesome: Munson, a sunset, and me.

I was nervous and didn't know what to say. "Have you ever been in love?" What in the world made me ask that?

He didn't even hesitate. "Once."

"What was her name?"

"Melanie."

"Melanie? She sounds helpless, like she catches a lot of colds," I remarked. Was I jealous, or was it envious? I couldn't remember the difference described in that psychology book on my mother's night table.

"Never sick a day!" he boasted. "She was in great shape." A grin.

"What was she like?" I couldn't care less.

"What a body!" A knowing look.

Deciding that was risky, I went on to something else.

"Why did you break up?" I guess that's what happened. Otherwise he wouldn't be here with me.

"She couldn't get enough." Another one of those looks.

"Oh." I made my face go blank. Did he mean what I thought he meant?

"She was so demanding, you'd think she was my wife. Wanted me to give up the debating team, resign from Key Club, stop working on the school newspaper." He reached out to touch my hair and then grabbed my hand. "No way! I need a free woman, a woman of the nineties!"

The warm wind blew around us in circles. "Of course," I nodded, surprised to hear about all those after-school activities. He must be more popular than I'd realized. Suddenly, Munson wasn't as short as he seemed. "And now?" I asked in a tender way. "Would you like to fall in love again?" Why couldn't I talk about anything else? TV? Tapes? Sneakers? Stephen King's latest?

"Sure, if she was more independent." His dark curls flopped in my direction. Raising his hips, he shifted his weight on the rock and moved closer to me. "And she'd better be sexy!" he whispered. "I've got one helluva sex drive!"

"That's nice." Not overly impressed, yet pleased, as if he'd just announced, "Look, no cavities!"

"One helluva sex drive!" he emphasized again. "How about you?"

"Me?" Meaning what? My sex drive?

"Have you ever been in love?" Munson asked.

What could I say? That I'd never been kissed? Not

really, not the kind that counts. That I was the other half of the nation's 15- to 19-year-old girls who have had premarital sex? I wasn't even the right statistic! He'd dump me if he knew. I had to invent. There was no other way. It took me only a minute. "There was once a pre-med student," I lied, lowering my eyes to study my nails.

"What was his name?"

"Anatole." Where had *that* come from?

"He sounds like a French poodle."

"He was a man, believe me! A real hunk!" Another Rambo?

"What was he like?"

"Handsome, brilliant, moody." An irresistible combination.

"Tall?" Munson looked unhappy.

Uh-oh. Better avoid that one. "He had three fingers missing from his left hand."

Munson shuddered. "What happened?"

"Research." Dropping my voice, I held up three fingers and glanced over to see if he was watching.

"But how?"

I hadn't the faintest idea. Using a scalpel? Caught in a tourniquet? "I never asked," I said, hoping to give the impression that such a question would have been in terrible taste.

Munson regarded me with awe.

I couldn't blame him. Anatole certainly brought out the best in me. I was really getting into it. "We'd stay up most of the night talking about commitment and compromise." Commitment and compromise. I liked that. Most of the night. I liked that, too.

Munson kicked pine needles from the rock. "Was it the first time, the first time you . . ." he blundered, making it worse as he added, "With only two fingers!"

I pretended not to understand as I looked down at the water.

"They say doctors make the best lovers," remarked Munson.

Was that true? I thought of my mother and father. He was only a dentist, but still. . . . I got as far as imagining them in the bathroom rinsing with Scope, then sitting on the edge of the bed, kicking off their slippers before turning to one another. Something in my head put an artist's palette and a dental pic on the mattress to separate them. Why couldn't I picture my parents having sex? I wondered. It made me squirm. I preferred making up stories about Anatole. "One day we went to the morgue," I said.

"A real hangout." Munson looked bored.

Now was the time to get rid of my pre-med student. "Anatole was given a grant to study in Tahiti."

Munson was impressed.

I couldn't resist one last detail. "He went deep-sea diving and sent me a pearl."

His jaw dropped. "Real?"

I nodded. "It's very valuable. I keep it in the vault along with my mother's diamond engagement ring." My voice turned sad. I'd miss Anatole.

We were quiet for a while. Munson was grieving over Melanie and I'd just lost Anatole.

"What about now?" Munson asked brightly. "Would you like to fall in love again?"

"Perhaps, in time," as if it didn't really matter. The truth was that I wanted to fall in love more than anything in the world and spent hours scribbling names like Keanu Reeves and Tom Cruise in my notebook.

We moved to another rock, a larger one. The sun was going down. With Anatole gone, I couldn't think of anything to say. I splashed water with my bare toes. Salt spray drenched my feet. A Coke bottle and bathing cap surfaced on the crest of a wave. I could feel Munson's body close to mine even though there were at least six inches between us. He smiled at me in a half-embarrassed kind of way. What was he thinking? The long silences were endless. Was it up to me to say something? His foot scratched mine underwater. I shivered.

"Cold?" he asked.

"No, I'm perfect."

He put his arm around me. I thought it would feel strange but it didn't. He inched over like an earthworm. I heard a rush of words, words like, "Please, please . . . I've never . . ." I didn't know what to do. I had no idea how it was supposed to be. Fingertips fumbled at my throat, straying inside my top. "Sunsets make me sexy," he said in a voice I'd never heard him use before. Suddenly, I was afraid of everything. Munson, myself, even the canteloupe-colored dusk.

"What are you thinking?" he wanted to know.

My heart answered. Surely he could hear? A bunch of dark curls came closer. His mouth was near. I wanted him to kiss me. I closed my eyes. We kissed. No one had ever told me how easy it was! We kissed again.

"Tell me what you're thinking," he whispered.

How could I? I'm happy, I might have replied, but if I said so, that happiness might go away. Maybe I hadn't earned it. How could I expect him — anyone — to understand?

Soon, a deeper kiss. My mouth parted. Without warning, a sharp stab on the inside of my lower lip. What on earth? Had Munson gone crazy? Bitten me in passion? How could he? He'd gone too far. He could have used a little more control.

"Maggie, what is it?" He pulled back.

A thorn of pain shot through my lower lip. Then I knew what had happened. "A metahaler!" I cried. "I need a metahaler!"

"A what?" Munson was annoyed. "For God's sake, Maggie, we're only kissing. You don't need any protection for that! Maybe later, when we . . ." His eyes widened. "You look terrible! You're ballooning! You should see you!"

My lip was swelling into a Frisbee. "It's a bee sting. I'm allergic to . . ." I couldn't manage any more details.

"Oh, my God!" Munson danced around in panic and nearly stumbled off the rock. "Don't you carry a kit or something?" He stiffened his back and tensed his shoulders. "You must have some pills!"

I shook my head. My parents would kill me! How often had they warned me never to forget my allergy medicine?

"I read somewhere that you have to get the stinger out. Now, where's the goddamned stinger?" Munson yanked open my mouth and peered inside as if he were combing the attic for a misplaced baseball glove. "The stinger's gone." Munson tried acting calm. "That's a good sign. Don't get hysterical! That's the worst possible thing. Keep your head! For God's sake, Maggie, keep your head!" He had no idea he was yelling. "This can only happen to me! Nothing ever goes right for me!"

I began to wheeze.

Munson helped me down from the rock and put a helmet on my head as he fastened his own. Lifting me on the seat of his moped, he zipped around corners, hardly braking through red lights until we reached the hospital. Every once in a while, he'd turn around and groan, mumbling something under his breath that sounded like, "Who needs this? Who needs this?"

I began to itch. Hives spread across my face as I held onto him and prayed for a long life.

"Mother's name?" We were at the admitting desk of the Emergency Room.

I stared at Munson, unable to answer because of my puffed lip.

"For God's sake!" he screamed. "What difference does it make? Look at her! Her lip is three times as big as it was! She can't even talk! Did you ever see such a mess?" Shaking his head in disbelief, he pointed to me for emphasis. "She's allergic to bees. With my luck, she could go into shock, maybe even die, for all I know. Anything's possible!"

"These are required forms," the volunteer persisted. "Mother's name?"

I reached over for a prescription pad and wrote on the top, Sara Gray.

"Maiden name?" the volunteer continued. "Living or dead? Insurance forms? Address? Winter? Summer? Allergies to penicillin? Whom to notify in case of emergency?"

Munson rolled his eyes and sighed.

Finally, a nurse appeared. Waving Munson toward the coffee machine, she led me through swinging doors, past stretchers and wheelchairs, to a room with a cot. After telling me to lie down, she pulled a curtain around me and said, "The doctor will be with you shortly."

My throat began to close. What if I stopped breathing? Within seconds, no more me. "The Lord is my Shepherd . . ." Whisperings at my funeral, "Poor girl, stung by a bee during a kiss! But why did she forget her pills?" My mother and father, too furious to mourn me, would rush back to the cottage to throw out my medicine and metahaler as Jenny helped herself from my jewelry box.

A doctor swung open the curtain and gave me a shot of Adrenalin. I inhaled, I exhaled. No more hissing in my chest! Munson would be so relieved. How worried he must have been! Poor Munson, probably a nervous wreck, pacing up and down, drinking gallons of coffee as he waited to hear if I was dead or alive. I pictured our reunion. We'd run into one another's arms. He'd go on and on about how brave I was and I'd thank him for saving my life and not phoning my parents. And then we'd get back on his moped, go to the rock, and finish what we'd started. "I promised you a sunset," he would say, pressing me hard against him. And I would . . .

The nurse re-appeared and told me I could leave.

Munson wasn't in the waiting room. I looked every-where. No one knew where he was. I found him outside leaning against his moped. When he saw me, he shouted, "For God's sake, Maggie, you've got some nerve! I could have been stuck with a corpse instead of a date!" He shoved a pair of goggles at me and yanked at the helmet. "I'm taking you home!"

I slung my leg over the back of his bike and got on the rear seat. He hit the pedal once again. We were off. He drove much too fast. It was so dark I could hardly see.

Dear Maggie,

I'm never going to be a Mother! I hate mine! She's a pain! First she makes me straighten my room up and says so what if theres a live in couple and a laundress. Then she wants to know what I'm planning to do with my life besides waste it. Before I can say a word she's putting on her leotard and spraying Destiny perfume all over to get ready for the exersize trainer who pays house calls. I was reading *Beverly Hills People* when I saw that Mike Nichols spent $430,000 dollars for a colt in Florida and that theres a big need for experts in the feild of horses. I went to the Library (beleive it or not Ha Ha) and theres something new called Equestrian Sciense. There are three colleges that give it. Ones in California and Wisconsin and Missouri. I got all excited and when I told my mother she said I was unrealistic and to take a typing and shorthand course because with my grades the best I can hope for is somebody's secretery. When I told Daddy about it he got a funny look on his face and said time will tell time will tell. He goes to the urologist every week with urine specamins. I didn't lose any weight as a matter of fact I gained one pound. The akupunturist said with a small percent sometimes it doesn't work. Ziggy moved a small T.V. into the barn and Midnight sniffs my hand and pockets for sugar. Then Ziggy kids around and does the same thing. We're a family. The three of us are great together!

xxxx yoyo ☺

P.S.   Munson sounds sexy.
P.P.S.   Dustin Hoffman is short, too, and so is Dudley Moore.

# SEVEN

A package was delivered to me the next day. It was an old shoe box with a red bow stuck on it. Inside were a bunch of chocolate M & M's with a card that read: M loves M! I'm sorry!

The telephone rang.

"Hi!" said Munson, "It's me! Did you get it?" He sounded happy, like a boy who'd won an award at camp.

"Yes."

"And?"

"I love presents!" I said.

"That's it? That's all?" He wanted more.

"Thank you."

"For what?" Still more.

"The M & M's, the sunset, you." I squeezed the receiver. "Everything!"

"Anything else?" Persistent.

"Munson . . ." I was embarrassed. M loves M! Is that what he was waiting for? Writing it was easier than

73

saying it. "You were pretty mad last night," I said.

"I was scared," he said. "I yell when I'm scared. It's a rotten habit of mine."

"It's scary to be scared," I said.

"Things are lousy. My parents are getting a divorce." Muffled, so that I could barely hear him, "I'm going to Chicago in the fall to live with my father."

"Oh, I'm sorry."

"I'll spend holidays back east with my mother."

"Oh, I'm sorry."

"I don't want anyone to know. Okay?"

"Sure."

"Did you tell your parents about the bee sting?"

"God, no! They were asleep when I got home," I said. "And don't *you* tell. Okay?"

"Sure."

In a telephone whisper, he said, "I meant what I wrote."

M loves M! I longed to say something but couldn't. Would I always be tongue-tied with feelings? I wondered. Suddenly, I noticed an oil painting propped against the wall. Sea-foam eyes and hair like freshly shucked corn. "Munson, I have to go," I said.

"You sound funny. You okay?"

"Talk to you later." I hung up. I had to see the canvas right away. The closer I got, the further away she seemed.

Colors splintered her complexion. Soft pastels tinted the right side. Dabs of brown stained the left. Her thin hand held a blue wildflower with falling petals. You knew, as you stared at the portrait, that soon only the stem would remain.

I heard my mother behind me. "What do you think?"

"Kimberley?" I had to be sure. It was even more abstract than anything my mother had ever done.

"Yes."

"But she's not smiling." Why was she painted that way? Pushed so far back into the distance that it made me afraid. I wanted to grab her and remind her of all the things we'd planned. "I can't wait to show you Manhattan," Kimberley had often said. "Sleepovers, gallery hopping in Soho, dim sum delicacies in Chinatown, a picnic in Central Park." I felt abandoned, somehow, as if she'd just phoned to break a date, giving a vague, unsatisfying excuse. Something was wrong, something hidden that alarmed me. Kimberley didn't look the same. That upset me. Things like that always bothered me. Change. It put me slightly off balance. "You took away her smile!" I accused my mother.

Her silence bewildered me.

I was used to my mother's art, that crazy part that drew unrelated objects such as a thimble, a bird cage, a teacup without a handle. But this was different. Another dimension I didn't understand.

"Why did Kimberley choose a wildflower?" I asked.

"There wasn't any flower," she replied.

"But you put it there!"

"Sometimes the brush takes over."

"What about the petals?"

She shrugged. "You know me, Maggie, how I work. It's not always what I see. At times, it's what I don't see."

"She looks sad."

"Yes," my mother agreed. "I'd rather talk about beauty. Does it touch you? Is it real?"

What was going on here? Where was my happiness? Since Kimberley, everything had been so perfect. I needed her now. I needed to be with her so much that I was scared.

"What is it, darling?" from my mother.

"When were you with her? Where was I?"

"She dropped over — why do you look like that? You were here that rainy afternoon when she suggested — "

" — She's *my* friend, not yours!" I pictured the two of them together. My mother would be asking Kimberley whether . . . perhaps? And Kimberley, in turn, would confide that. . . . Would they talk of me?

"Yes, darling, of course she's your friend, but . . ." She came closer.

What was in her mind? I didn't ask. I was afraid to hear anything that might disturb me. "Don't touch me! Stay away!" I stepped back. "You've always interfered!" It wasn't true. It wasn't true at all. "You're in the way," I said.

She dropped her head for a moment. I'd hurt her. Good!

"Stay out of my life!" I screamed. I couldn't believe how cruel I was. Yet, at that moment I had to hate her! I had to hate her frizzy hair, the gold molar that twinkled at her throat, her baggy jeans and dirty sneakers. Why? I wasn't sure. I'd always trusted her, relied on her to kiss and make it better. Now, she was taking Kimberley away from me. It was her fault that I was suddenly miserable. Confused and guilty, I heard myself say once again, "Stay out of my life!" horrified because it gave me pleasure and pain, like picking at a scab.

"Be careful, Maggie, be careful," her voice as loving as when I was a little girl and she warned me to look both ways before crossing the street. Did she know something I didn't? One day, I told myself, this would be less mysterious. Kimberley and my mother. My mother and Kimberley.

I glanced at the portrait once again. I made my imagination pick up the falling petals and put back Kimberley's smile.

Dear Maggie,

This will be short because I'm busy with place cards for a huge affair katered by Chasens. Its a real zoo here with Alfred washing the windows and Denny painting the trim and pool guys fixing the filter and the piano tuner tuning and Hattie ironing tablecloths and Maria and Pabloe are in a bad mood because its to much silver polishing and to much company and to late hours. The cast of Beverly Hills 90210 are coming. And Eddie Murphy with his new Porsh and Robert Mitchum who never comes to parties and Brooke Sheilds without her mother. Mommy went to an auction to bid on signed autographs of Greta Garbo and Marilyn Monroe and Marlene Deitrich for dance prizes and Daddys at the doctors. The florist just phoned to say they're on there way over with orchids to float in the pool and can anyone sign? Gotta go now! My mother said to be sure to check the safe inside the movie projecter in case of burglery.

xxxx yo yo 🙂

P.S.   Your new freinds sound great!
P.P.S.   Sometimes its easier talking to Ziggy and Midnight then selebrities.

# EIGHT

"$H$ow was your date with Munson?" Kimberley asked me a few days later as we were sitting on the lawn waiting for everyone to arrive for a barbecue.

"He kissed me," I said. "I kissed him back."

She smiled.

I didn't say anything else. The part about Munson loving me. I wasn't sure why. I couldn't get him out of my mind. The way his eyes fell into mine. It was almost the same look that Zach gave Kimberley. Each morning, I'd awaken, thinking, Munson, Munson, Munson.

Jenny chose that moment to share some brownies she'd baked. Sensing that something important was going on, she sat on the grass and didn't budge.

My father was scrubbing the grill. He looked happy, as if he were getting ready to fill a cavity. He was thinking: It's about time Maggie invited her new friends over.

My mother was in the kitchen frowning over a cookbook, figuring out how to double the noodle casserole recipe for six. She was thinking: Globs of paint are easier.

Eloise ran over. Her nose was shiny as black patent leather. Her small ears flopped. We'd decided not to dock them like most Schnauzers because it reminded my mother of Van Gogh, the artist who cut off one of his own. Eloise lay on her belly with her head resting between graying paws. One strand of her beard grew the wrong way like a cowlick. The cataract in her left eye was milky.

"Is Munson your *boy*friend?" Jenny asked, getting straight to the point.

I ignored her.

Kimberley was playing with a buttercup that she held under her chin. "Do you see yellow?" she asked Jenny. "That means I love butter."

"Not margarine?" wisecracked Jenny.

I began to daydream. Listening to the whirling wheels of the windmill, I wondered if there had been another girl — a century ago — like me? Did she wish that she understood life? Did she open the dormer window and look out beyond the meadow where the deer came up? Could she smell the salt from the harbor? Pick huckleberries for dessert? At night, would she wait for the wail of gulls? In the morning, would she pick a wild rose for someone special? What was his name? Was his first initial M?

Soon there were bikes in the driveway. As usual, everyone paired off. Kimberley and Zach were helping my father. Toby and Bimbo disappeared into the kitchen with my mother. Jenny was talking about me with Clipper and Snow. "It's cool that Maggie and Munson are messin' around!" I overheard her say. Munson and I were unexpectedly awkward with each other.

Two redwood tables covered with blue-and-white-checked cloths were pushed together in the backyard. "How lovely!" Kimberley said, so quietly that she might have been talking to herself. She seemed overcome, close to tears. How strange, I remember thinking. What was so unusual about paper napkins, an over-sized pepper grinder, wooden plates, and stoneware mugs?

"It's only a barbecue," I said.

"Oh, no, Maggie, it's much more! It's family!" She was slightly breathless. "Nothing in my life was ever like this!"

I didn't say that it sounded extreme, all out of proportion. I didn't say anything.

My parents sat at opposite ends of the table so that they could exchange glances, sum up everything between them. Munson put his hand on my knee under the table, taking it away only to smear mustard on his frank. Kimberley seemed restless. She looked oddly flushed. At first, she'd listen to my father, her profile toward him. Then she'd shift, her movements somewhat jerky, her perfect hands trembling. Staring ahead, she gazed at me as if she didn't see me, absorbed in something, silent one moment, animated the next. Resting her chin between palms in that way of hers, she removed herself. I could feel it. About to take off, destination unknown. Whispering, "Excuse me," she got up.

Was I supposed to follow? I was afraid of doing the wrong thing. Did she need to be alone or was she waiting for me? I wanted to please her. If it weren't for Kimberley, I'd still be on the outside of things. Because of her, I felt singled out.

What if she were sick? Another one of her headaches?

I followed her into the house and knocked on the bathroom door.

"Come in." She was closing her silver pillbox, putting the brown bottle into her bag. Her hair was pulled back into a knot, which exaggerated the bones of her cheeks. Her neck and shoulders were rigid inside her white shirt.

"What's wrong? Tell me!"

"Nothing's wrong," she said coldly.

"Don't do that! Don't push me away!"

"Oh, Maggie," was all she said. She had that hazy look she got sometimes. What was happening inside her head? There were times when I could read her mind. I knew, for instance, that when her green eyes darkened, she was hiding something. Twisting a strand of hair around a finger meant that she was fantasizing. If her voice dropped, she was tearful. And to hide terror, she turned flip. But sometimes, she bewildered me. Suddenly, she crumpled, slumping over the toilet seat. "My world is . . ." she mumbled so that I couldn't hear.

I kneeled down on the tiled squares and put my arms around her. "Headaches? Migraine?" I could cope with that. It was something I was used to.

"I'm low, real low."

"But why?"

"A carousel, up and down, round and round. Where's the gold ring?" speaking too quickly. Making no sense. Was she high? Did she do drugs? But she would have told me. I was her close friend. She told me so.

I got up, pulling her with me so that we could both sit on the edge of the bathtub.

"I'm so tired, I could sleep forever. Would you wake me, Maggie, after forever?" she said.

I hadn't the faintest idea what she was talking about. And then I heard her say softly, ever so softly, "I'm scared."

"Scared? YOU?" disbelieving, incredulous. "YOU?" again, not really wanting to listen to any more.

Swiftly, fingertips brushed my cheek. "Are you always true blue? No dirty smudges?"

What on earth did she mean?

I didn't dare ask. "I need them . . . they help me."

Them? They?

"There's something I've got to tell you. . . ." Kimberley hesitated, on the verge of saying more.

Nothing was making sense. Something was bad. I didn't want to know. It was more than I could bear. If I changed the subject it would go away. Step over the crack and no bad luck. "There's coffee ice cream for dessert, my favorite," I rattled on. If I'd said something else, something more like, "Tell me everything!" it might have been different. But I didn't.

She tried to smile. "You won't tell anyone?"

I still wasn't sure that I understood.

"Promise me."

"I promise. I *promise!*" I'd do anything for her. Nothing could ever make me break that vow. If there was anything seriously wrong, I'd have guessed.

Moments later, we went back outside. Kimberley sat beside my father. What was she saying? I tried to make out her words. Did she like him? We could share him. I wouldn't mind. At another time, I might tell her that.

My mother was talking to Snow. "No, I've never had my own art show. I'd like to, someday, but I'm not ready yet." I was surprised to hear her confiding things she never told anyone except her family. "Beautiful art must give the truth," she explained with a smile that I was certain was meant for me. She was referring, I knew, to Kimberley's portrait. Then, as if concerned at having revealed too much, she turned to Toby and offered her more noodles.

"How do you define success?" my father was asking everyone. It was a favorite family topic.

"Having my ears pierced!" piped in Jenny, who should have known better. She'd been told a million times that she'd have to wait until she was older.

We talked about what we wanted to do with our lives.

Snow thought for a while before saying, "I'm happy when I'm with my goldfish."

"Goldfish?" we all said at the same time.

He went on, "I've got four tanks filled with orange

and calico fish sliding around. They wait for me and know when it's time to be fed. No overcrowding, no overeating, they need me." Snow could never sit still. He got up and walked around the tables before sitting down again. "Maybe I'll be a vet," he said.

My parents smiled together. If they had alarm clock transplants, the buzzers would go off simultaneously.

— "My family is rich," broke in Zach who was shaking ketchup onto his third hamburger. "Success means the best of everything: camps, schools, report cards." He paused to ask for the relish. "So far I've done rather well." He speared an onion and took a bite of pickle. Grinning, he added, "Maybe it's time for me to rebel."

"Music is everything!" remarked Bimbo, staring at his long fingernail.

Toby said that she probably wouldn't go to college and might even end up as a waitress for a caterer.

"Success is seven hundred on the verbal, six-fifty on the math," said Clipper, who was wearing a large sombrero. She always protected her pale complexion against the sun.

"I haven't the faintest idea what success is or how it applies to me," Munson said after he'd put his hot dog down.

"Me neither! Me too!" I squeezed Munson's hand.

That left Kimberley. She was the only person who hadn't spoken. "Love," she said, finally.

Hers was the best! I thought.

Eloise began sniffing at my sneaker. She stared at

me as if trying to tell me something. I leaned down to pet her. She ran around in circles. Everyone laughed. Was it a game? A trick? She tried to catch her tail. Jumping into the air, her dark eyes never left mine as she leaped higher and higher. I lunged for her. Eloise was having another epileptic seizure! My father stretched out his arms to make a circle with mine. My mother had already run inside for the Dilantin. Quickly, she pried open Eloise's mouth and shoved a pill down her throat.

"Will she die?" Jenny asked.

Silence. We were all afraid of saying the wrong thing.

"She's not going to die, is she?" Jenny cried. "Please, Daddy, don't let her die!"

I'll never forget my father's reply. "She's all right now, Jenny, but none of us is here forever."

Everyone became fidgety. "David," said my mother. Not, "Darling." "Sara," said my father. Not, "Honey." That meant they were nervous. I thought of my grandmother who took off her high-heeled pumps before crawling into bed to die. "Am I dying?" she'd whispered to my mother who said, "No! No!" and later confessed that she'd never forgiven herself for lying.

Clipper broke the tension by suggesting that we go to her place and play with her new Ouija board. I wasn't sure about leaving Eloise.

"All she needs now is a nap," my mother reassured me.

"I'll read Judy Blume to her," said Jenny.

Just then, someone asked, "Where's Kimberley?"

We looked around.

*Snap. Snap.* I could almost hear the pillbox closing. "She had to make a phone call," I said. *Snap. Snap.*


Clipper's house was on a hill overlooking the bay. There were flowers everywhere, even on the chintz covering the sofa and chairs. The living room had large glass windows. We sat around a table on the outside terrace. Lanterns gave off enough light for us to read the letters and numbers on the Ouija board. I'd never seen one before. On the upper left, there was a drawing of the sun smiling. Nearby was the word *yes.* On the upper right was the crescent of a moon. Near that was *no.* At the bottom, *good-bye* was written.

"How do we play?" Snow wanted to know. "Everyone ask a different question?"

Zach suggested that we choose only one.

"Okay, what's the question?"

"Who'll ask me to the prom? How long will I be a virgin?" giggled Clipper as she flirted with Snow.

"Virgin? What's that?" Bimbo teased.

"Madonna's new perfume!" replied Toby.

"Come on, be serious," warned Zach. "Poke fun at the occult and it won't work."

Kimberley took over and came up with, "What do the fates have in store for me?"

Tarot cards and fortunes . . . a poltergeist . . . spirit rapping and table tipping . . . a séance . . . ghosts and spirits all around.

They were really getting into it.

"I'm scared," I said, and meant it. It was a mistake. The Who Cares all stared at me, unwilling to stop joking and laughing. After a while, I joined in. It was sort of funny. Besides, I didn't want to be kicked out of their group. Their special club.

Bimbo turned the board so that the letters faced him. "What do the fates have in store for me?" he asked, resting his long fingernail on the disc. It went to R, then O, traveling to C, ending with K. "Rock! That proves it! Music's my life! What did I tell you?" He relaxed, triumphant.

"You pushed the letters! Anyone can do that," Kimberley said. She never looked prettier. Everything about her had softened: her hair, her shoulders, even her eyes. If her picture had been snapped at that very moment, it would have been enlarged into a glossy for her modeling portfolio. She even threw back her head and laughed. I was convinced there was nothing more to worry about.

Toby followed. The disc landed on A, then C, N, E. Acne. Oh, no. We were all embarrassed as Toby went into a dreary monologue explaining how her dermatologist prescribed tetracycline, but it made her sick to her stomach.

Kimberley said that her skin broke out sometimes, too.

"Really?" Toby felt much better.

I was positive Kimberley never had a zit in her life.

Clipper's turn. The disc skipped the top letters, zipped over the numbers and settled on *goodbye*.

"But what does it mean?" She was worried.

"It's only a game," reassured Kimberley. "Trust me, there's no shining oracle inside."

"Right!" agreed Snow, whose letters spelled out B-A-B-I-E-S. "My goldfish! The female's having her babies! I had no idea it would be this soon!" He was upset, almost frantic.

"Natural childbirth?" Bimbo kidded.

Snow paid no attention to him. "This is unbelievable! How does it — "

" — You controlled it!" Munson insisted.

"No, I swear." Snow held up his right hand.

"Someone is sending and receiving messages," Zach said. Then, in a solemn voice, he asked, "What do the fates have in store for me?" He waited, then was puzzled at the reply, S-P-A-C-E. He couldn't figure it out. "Space?" he frowned.

"Leaving me for the moon?" Kimberley stared up at the sky.

It was Munson's turn. D-A-D. He shot me a look. Had I told anyone about our phone conversation, his parent's divorce?

I shook my head. Of course not. That was between us.

But he seemed doubtful.

"Dad! Father of the new goldfish, Munson?" asked Snow.

"Pervert!" scolded Clipper.

It continued that way. It was important to have fun. We were all getting a little jittery.

I wanted to get it over with. What about my fate? I

wondered. I prayed for something silly. Then we could all relax. Nothing prepared me for P-E-T-A-L. It was eerie. My mother's portrait of Kimberley. What else could it be? Those petals that fell from the blue wild-flower haunted me. I saw the way Kimberley's eyes narrowed. Was she angry with me? Was it something I did? Something I said? Didn't say? We'd never dis-cussed those hours she spent alone with my mother. How can I explain it? There was something dark. I gave up trying to understand. "Petal?" I said. "I haven't the faintest idea — "

Kimberley yanked the board from me. "So, Mister Magic, tell me! I'm listening!" She acted bold, as if it didn't matter, but I knew that her heart was beating as fast as anyone else's. The disc seemed uncertain, weav-ing in and out, down to numbers, back up to letters, as if waiting for some mysterious command. Finally, G-L-O-W, which had us baffled. "Glow," Kimberley snickered. "Probably a new Revlon product, blusher maybe, or lip gloss." She folded the board and gave it back to Clipper. "So much for spooks!"

She was right, of course. She always was. We slumped back in our chairs. It was getting humid. Mos-quitoes buzzed. There were no stars. Clipper and Kim-berley went inside for Cokes and potato chips. The stereo was turned on loud so that we could hear it outside. Vivaldi? Schubert? Classical music reminded me of my grandmother who played the piano with jade and coral rings on her fingers. "Who's the composer?" she used to quiz me. I concentrated now. It was familiar, yet . . . ? Why was it so important that I recognize it? I wondered. Mozart? Liszt?

If only, I thought, this summer would never end. Sand pebbles, unbroken seashells, the salt smell of the tide. The Who Cares — being together was like riding a perfect wave. Must everything change? How often would Kimberley and I see one another once school began? I'd invite her for Thanksgiving and she could have the drumstick. Christmas? Her stocking hanging next to mine. I'd wheeze during February's flu and address valentines with dangling hearts and cherubs to "My Best Friend."

Suddenly, "My God! What's that?" Bimbo was pointing to something white fluttering outside a window.

We watched as if dreaming. Unreal, faraway, it had nothing to do with us . . . until we realized, with horror, that something terrible was happening. Was it — ? No, impossible. A curtain rimmed in flames? We raced inside the house calling for Clipper who, until then, was busy in the kitchen with no idea of what was going on. We hurried after her as she ran screaming along the hallway. One bedroom had an unmade bed. Where were Clipper's parents? I wondered, wishing for the grown-ups to take charge. There was another room. Smoke rolled in from under a closed door. It was getting hotter and hotter. I felt the way I did when I got too much sun at the beach.

"Open up, Kimberley! Let us in!" Clipper shouted, as she kicked the door open. Sitting on the floor, yoga-style, was Kimberley who seemed dazed, as if aroused from a deep sleep. Nearby, in a saucer with a puddle of melted wax, was an overturned candle. What in the world had she been doing? My eyes burned as I began to cough, swallowing down nausea. Zach and Munson stomped on the flames. I staggered around. HEY! YOU IN THERE! my thoughts went wild as I blamed the Ouija board. IT'S ALL YOUR FAULT! HER WORD. . . . G-L-O-W. PRESTO! A FIRE!

It crackled. The blaze spiraled. Clipper yelled, "Water! A pail!" as we pulled down the soot-dusted curtains. The room was flooded in brilliance, orange, pink, and yellow strobe lights shooting everywhere. Kimberley was still, as if sculpted. Furious, I wanted to shake her! Instead, I grabbed her to me as if to reassure myself that she was still there, that she'd always be there. She smelled like Papa, my grandfather, who smoked too many cigarettes even after he was warned. She clung to me, her white shirt as scorched as an ironing-board cover. "Are you all right?" I cried over and over again, startled to see her eyes cloud over in a way that took me right back to Eloise.

"Fire! Fire!" Finally, someone was on the telephone.

"Are you all right?" once more, as I watched her come out of it.

"Where am I? . . . meditating . . . Why am I here?" She looked tired and confused.

Zach wrapped a blanket around her and dashed through the hallway, past the kitchen, back onto the terrace. He held Kimberley like he would a child as he breathed life back into her. I'd never seen them so close. That image was like a curtain separating them from me. I longed to put myself inside the blanket so that I, too, could feel the things she did.

There were sirens. Red lights blinked through shrubs.

Later, we learned that the firemen had arrived just in time.

I couldn't believe Kimberley's off-handed remark to us. "If you have to die, you might as well do it to Chopin's Sonata for Piano #2 in B-flat!"

She knew! Even then she knew!

That night I had my dream again.

I was still trapped in the cellar.

*Dear Maggie,*

*Are you OK? What about Kimberley? I haven't heard from her recently. Your letter about the fire was scary! How did it begin? We used to have a ouija board before we got computers. Kimberleys word was wierd. What was yours? You didn't say. I have a funny feeling your not telling me everything. I wish we lived closer. I need your advice! It's hard writing this but its imperetive! My feelings for Ziggy are getting intense but I can't handle it. The other night he got mad and called me a tease. I'm crazy about him but how do you know if your really in love? Its great having a boy friend and kissing but the rest scares me and I think maybe theres something wrong and I'm frigid. SEX is on my mind NIGHT AND DAY. There are twins down the street who have SEX every Saturday night. Everybody says everybodys doing it but I wonder. Could you phone me and tell me what you and Munson do? I mean how far does he try? Its none of my buziness but your the only one I can ask. Not Kimberley because shes to sofisticated. Hurry I'm desperate because I'm afraid Ziggy will find someone else who won't say no. Call me anytime collect. You have my unlisted number. Don't worry no one can listen. I have a private phone in my bathroom.*

*xxxx yo yo* ☺

*P.S.   If you don't want to tell me its OK I'll improvize.*
*P.P.S.   Is Eloise alright?*
*P.P.P.S.   I knew a girl in the fifth grade who had epilepsy and took Dilantin and shes great now!*

# NINE

The days went slowly for me. I'd been restless ever since the fire.

One evening Munson and I were walking. "Things go wrong," he said, glancing down at his bare feet. "Things you never dreamed about." He was referring to his parents.

"But if you're close to someone, you know everything. If something's wrong, you feel it," I said.

"It figures."

"What figures?"

"You see everything the way you want to."

"That's not true!"

"Life isn't that simple." He sounded self-important.

"I guess you know more about life than I do," I said.

"Maybe." He agreed in a way that annoyed me. Stepping over a piece of glass on the road, he said, "Do you know what it's like to have your father walk out? To be afraid that he's leaving because of you. That he

95

might not give a damn?" For a second, I thought Munson was reaching out to touch me. Instead, he slapped a mosquito on my neck. "Do you have any idea what that's like?"

"No, I don't know what it's like," I had to admit. "But maybe he'll come back. Maybe your mother and father will get together again."

Munson shook his head. "There you go again."

"Love doesn't just go away." I believed this at the time.

"Honestly, Maggie, how come you're so naive?"

"I believe in wishing, that's all." I was getting huffy.

"Wishing . . . I'll have to give that a try." His voice was hoarse. For a minute I thought he was going to break down and cry. "First separation, then divorce," he said. "I'm not sure I have enough going with my Dad to move to Chicago with him."

"I'm sorry," I said.

He rubbed his cheek. "You're sorry?"

"Yes."

"What do you mean?"

"Nothing," I said. Then, "Would you rather stay here with your mother?"

He forced a smile. "And lose my macho image?"

It was getting dark. The stores were closing. There was a line outside the seafood restaurant. A naked little boy ran from his house. A dog barked. I squeezed Munson's hand. If only I could make him less unhappy. It wasn't fair that his parents were living apart. Munson didn't deserve to be lonely.

"I can't get the fire out of my mind," he said suddenly.

"My parents phoned Clipper's mother and father to ask if they could do anything."

"Weren't they furious? Mine would have been, if I'd told them, if they were still together."

Fireflies lit the dusk as I said, "They were worried about all of us, especially Kimberley. But mostly, they were grateful that we were okay."

"Sometimes, I wake up in the middle of the night . . ."

"But we're safe!" I reminded him.

"There was something about Kimberley that night . . . something. . . . She was so . . ." He tried to find the right word.

I wasn't sure that I wanted to hear. I was hoping that the name Kimberley would be dropped. "Beautiful?" I knew that wasn't what he meant. I was afraid to look at his face.

". . . something I've never noticed before."

I had to change the subject. I couldn't talk about Kimberley with him, with anyone. "Let's go back to the rock, the same one," I suggested, knowing that he'd be pleased.

He leaned forward, his curls dancing in anticipation as he said, "Exactly what *I* was thinking!"

We rolled up our jeans before wading out. The water was freezing as we climbed onto the rock. Munson held out his arms. "This is our rock," he said. "Our special rock." I smiled to myself as he stroked my cheek and gathered me to him, kissing my hair, my mouth. I kissed him tenderly at first, then harder, much harder. I tried to make up for his mother and father who made him

miserable by divorcing. Or was I kissing him that way
because I wanted to make him stop talking about Kimberley? Then I felt his fingertips sliding down the inside
of my top. I grabbed his wrist and pushed his hand
away. "Don't! Please don't!" I cried.

"I thought you cared!"

"I do."

"Listen, Maggie, don't you want to?"

I stared at a candy wrapper skimming the waves. I
watched it coming up, going under, as salt wind stung
my eyes. I suppose I'm not sure, I told myself. For a
moment, I was silent.

Munson jumped down and strode through the water
toward the beach. I saw the bright stripes of his polo
shirt move like caterpillars in the night. "Coming, Maggie?" he called over his shoulder.

I was afraid. What if he dropped to his knees and
pulled me down beside him? What would I do? I was
terrified of being found, discovered under a crescent of
moon, by someone who would tell my parents. I heard
voices in my head.

Father: "Beware of the everybodies!"

Mother: "Don't forget your allergy pills!"

Jenny: "Is he your *boy*friend?"

God: "Shame on you!"

Quickly, I slid off the rock to follow Munson.

"You drive me crazy!" he said, reaching for me.

"Why?"

"I love touching you. You feel so smooth."

"Oh," as I hugged him.

"I could touch you forever, non-stop."

"Really?"

Holding me tight, he sniffed my scalp and said, "Your hair squeaks. Do you wash it every day or every other?" His weight shifted as he sat on the sand. "And your eyes, such huge pupils — like you just came back from the eye doctor."

I sat opposite him and kept looking at my lap. Was this the way Zach complimented Kimberley? I wondered. I couldn't imagine *him* talking about shampoo or eyedrops. And how would she reply, if he did? She'd say something clever, something I wished I could think of.

"I've memorized you," Munson continued. "Your hair, your eyes, your lips, your breasts . . ."

I couldn't believe this.

Grinning, he said, "I like the way your lipstick smears. I like the way your shirt sticks out. I like the way you're not perfect." And then, "Look up at the moon, Maggie."

I did.

"What do you see?"

I shrugged. "The moon."

Munson seemed disappointed. "He's giving us his blessing, telling us to go ahead."

I imagined Kimberley once again and could almost hear her saying, "*He*? The moon's a he? Why not a she?"

"You make me feel tall," Munson went on. "Much taller than I really am." Slowly, he tightened his biceps, preening, so that I could see his muscles. "Five-foot-seven, maybe. You're my multi-vitamin."

"From A to Zinc?" There. Wasn't I funny? That was something Kimberley might have said.

"You won't change, Maggie? Chicago won't make a difference?"

"No." I really believed I wouldn't change.

"What if you find someone taller than me?"

"I won't," I consoled him. "Besides, you're still growing."

"I'm an inch shorter than you."

It was more than an inch. Why quibble? I didn't want to hurt Munson. We were still sitting on the sand. He, with his legs tucked under him. Me, leaning back, my legs stretched out, crossed at the ankles. He was staring at me, eyes shining like a cat stalking his prey. Soon he would pounce.

"Tell me about your mother." I hoped to divert him.

"She reminds me of you. She's pretty but she doesn't think so." He put one paw in front of the other. "Teaches kindergarten."

"And your father? What does he do?" I rushed on.

"He travels a lot, selling panty hose. When he's home, he writes up orders. We don't talk much."

"Reinforced toe?"

"What?"

"The panty hose," I explained. "My mother says the sandalfoot doesn't last."

"Come here, Maggie." His hands glided over me. I had goosebumps as he pressed himself against me. I stiffened and felt feverish, first hot, then cold. I was confused. Was this really me, Maggie Gray? Or me trying to be someone else? Who was I, after all? A teenager trying to be popular? Or a young girl afraid of growing up? It felt so nice in his arms. Part of me longed for what everybody in school talked about all the time. Another part admitted that it wasn't what I wanted at all. I liked kissing and touching, especially the love-words. But I wasn't ready to have sex. Was something wrong with me? If I stopped Munson now, I might lose him. I'd die if that happened.

"I want you," he whispered. He stretched out lengthwise, patting a place on the sand for me.

"Munson, please. . . ." But in spite of myself I lay down next to him. Was this the correct way? I wondered. On my side? My back? I rested my face on his soft shirt.

At once he moved and spoke my name, "Maggie." His breath was too quick. He tried to slow it.

"When you hold me . . ." I didn't care that I was trembling.

"What?" he said. "When I hold you . . . what?"

Why was I suddenly so uncertain? Munson and I needed each other. We belonged together that summer. But something told me not to go on. I sat up and said, "I can't."

He sat up, too. "But why, Maggie, why?"

How could I tell him the reason when I didn't know myself?

"I thought you felt the same as me," he said.

"I do! Honest! But I just can't!" I turned away from him. Tears.

"Maggie, you're the only thing that's good in my life." His hand, gritty with pebbles, covered mine.

The air had turned cool. Waves rolled in heavy against our rock. Crickets sang in the dark grass. "Please don't hate me," I said.

Even in the night, I could see Munson's face crumple. He stood up slowly, wiping away a grease stain on his jeans from his moped. "It's okay," he said. "No big deal."

Head bowed, shoulders hunched, he could have been a broken toy soldier marching up the strip of wet sand to the lantern-lit street. "C'mon, Maggie," he called out to me. "I'll walk you home."

No one understood him. That's what he was thinking. I knew because I often felt that way myself. He was alone, all alone. There was no one. Not even the girl he trusted. Would he ever forgive me?

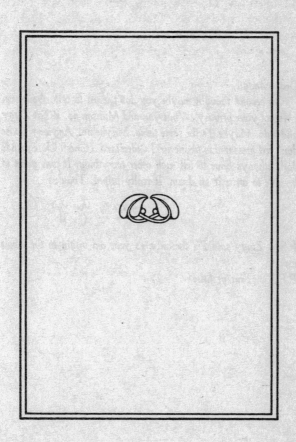

*Dear Maggie,*

*On second thought maybe you don't want to talk about sex. I respect your privasy. What you and Munson do. What Ziggy and I do. Maybe it's the same thing. Maybe not. Anyway please don't feel pressured to phone me. I understand. Honest! Close freinds don't always have to tell each other everything. It was great to be able to write it all down. It really helped. Thanks!*

xxxx yo yo ☺

*P.S. Ziggy said I'm the only 15 year old virgin in the whole world.*

*P.P.S. True or false?*

# TEN

In Menemsha, the wind blew, filling the air with specks of sand. Summer was going by too quickly. A Monday . . . a Wednesday . . . a Friday . . . and again, a Monday. . . . Days tucked inside one another. One August afternoon Kimberley and I were on our way to my house after shopping. Shampoo, emery boards, mosquito repellent. When we were together, I wished, the way a child wishes, that such moments would go on and on.

An ice cream truck rolled down the street. Kimberley reached into her pocket. "What would you like?" she asked me, taking out change.

The ice cream man eyed her before asking what flavor she wanted.

"Strawberry," she said. "Do you have strawberry?" Peeling off the paper, she held the stick toward me.

I took a small bite.

Then she finished it, licking her fingers.

The ice cream man was flirting as he winked at Kimberley. Opening the freezer, he laughed loudly and asked if she'd like something else. For free?

Anyone but Kimberley would have blushed and giggled. But she ignored him, tossing the wooden stick into nearby poison ivy.

What I felt for her was more than friendship. It had to do with love and, always, envy. "Oh, Kimberley," I said, "teach me to be like you!"

She looked at me as if she didn't understand. "You're happy, aren't you?"

"Yes . . . no . . . sometimes."

"But you're happy most of the time?"

"I guess so."

"Well, then," she said, "you're happy."

Yes, I thought, she must be right, and fell silent.

In my room, she told me that she was going away for a week. "My agency phoned," she explained, one hand fiddling with points of a silk scarf she'd knotted around her tiny waist. "They want me for a fashion shoot at Club Med."

"Don't go," I said.

"It's my job."

"Which Club Med?" I'd seen the TV commercials and heard about the wild parties at some of them.

"Eleuthera," she replied.

"I don't even know where that is."

"Somewhere in the Bahamas."

I pictured her dancing with men wearing loin cloths. "I don't want you to go!" I cried, throwing myself on the bed.

"I've taken a lot of time off, Maggie. Angela will kill

me if I don't get back to work." Leaning across my dresser, she smiled at a snapshot taken of Jenny holding Eloise. Then she went on to describe Club Med's gorgeous beach, jogging, water skiing, tennis, even an Olympic-sized swimming pool.

Would she miss me? I wondered, as I imagined her snorkling and playing with schools of fish.

She seemed in one of her brighter moods. I took it as a sign to stop listening for the snap of a closing pillbox. Kimberley was ravishing in torn jeans and a red tee. It was time for me to forget an overturned candle in a saucer. What was the point of dwelling on nightmares?

"Eleuthera comes from *eleutheria*, the Greek word for freedom," I heard her say.

Who cared? "Martha's Vineyard has freedom, too!" I pointed out.

Then she began telling me about all the free wine at lunch and dinner.

"Big deal," I said. "Anyway, you're under age."

"You pay for everything with beads."

"Beads? That's stupid." I was getting sulky.

"Piña coladas and — have you ever had one? All white and frothy."

I was reminded of a ballerina. "Like a tutu?"

"Oh, Maggie," she laughed, before remarking, "I love flying!"

"I hate flying." We'd never disagreed on anything before.

"But it's the closest you can get to heaven!" She opened my closet and went through my clothes. Pulling out my favorite sweatshirt, the faded one that skimmed my knees, she asked if she could borrow it.

"Sure!" I liked the idea of Kimberley wanting something of mine. At least part of me would be with her, I told myself.

"There's just one thing . . ." she hesitated.

"What?"

"Zach and I have been together so much this summer. I hate leaving him. Sometimes a week can be a long time."

How to reply? I thought seven days was an awful long time, but I wasn't sure if I was thinking of Kimberley and Zach or Kimberley and me.

"Do me a favor, Maggie. See that he keeps busy, okay?" she said. "I'm lucky, Zach and I trust one another. Like you and me, Maggie. We trust one another, don't we?" She pressed her hands together in that familiar way, making a steeple with her fingers. "I'll see you when I get back. We'll have a sleepover in New York."

I couldn't say that I already felt terribly alone. I tried to blink away the image of Kimberley in my sweatshirt, beads in her hand, having fun with new friends, a photographer, perhaps, and another model, someone she'd met on the plane, yelping with laughter as they sat on bar stools and sipped tutus through a single straw.

"I wish you could come with me," Kimberley said.

Did that mean she'd miss me?

"We'd giggle at the G.O.'s," she said.

"The G.O.'s? Something to do with government?"

"The staff. That's what they're called."

"Like camp counselors?"

"Only nude."

"Naked?" Was she serious? "Without any clothes?" That part wasn't on TV.

"Well, they carry trays." She was teasing. She had to be! Now, she was trying on my shoes. They were too big. Reaching for a bag at the back of my closet, she tested the zipper to see if it worked. "May I take this, too?" She really wasn't thinking of me.

"Nothing's the same without you," I confessed.

She squinted at me, smiling. "You have Munson and all the others, The Who Cares." Then she rushed on, "Three and a half hours on a plane doesn't change anything." She seized my wrist and squeezed it. "We're fated to be close friends, Maggie, ever since that day we had lunch with YoYo."

"Yes," I said, remembering that first time we met. I never told Kimberley how much I hated her then, how snooty I thought she was.

"We'll be friends for a long, long time . . . forever!" she said in a whisper.

Kimberley was in Eleuthera, probably fast asleep. I'd gotten up early. My mother was filling the coffeepot. "When is Kimberley coming back?" she asked, using that veiled voice whenever she spoke of her. I didn't answer. Something told me not to confide in my mother. She never pried or asked ordinary questions. Where did Kimberley go to school? What did her mother do? How long had she been dating Zach? But there was something separating us, something that was never there before. "Cereal?" She poured cornflakes into a bowl for me. I shook my head, silent, as once again I thought of Kimberley's portrait, a sadness painted on the canvas. "Sometimes the brush takes over," my mother had said to me. I didn't understand. What did the brush tell her? What did she know that I didn't?

"Is anything wrong, Maggie?"

"No. Why?"

"Would you like to invite some friends from home for a weekend?"

"No."

"You always used to."

"I don't feel connected to them."

"We don't talk anymore. Not like we used to. Something's on your mind. I know you." She looked at me, wanting me to air my feelings.

"No, you don't!" I said. "You don't know me at all!" and thought, Why doesn't she let me be?

"I love you," my mother called after me as I went down to the beach where I walked along the water's edge.

Sea gulls surfaced above the ocean. A sandpiper hopped in front of me. Want to race? he seemed to ask.

"Shut up!" I replied. I was far away with Kimberley. "I miss her! I miss her!" I spoke to the dawn. My feet made imprints on the damp sand. Stepping down harder, I tried to make them as sharp as the flatfooted sandpiper's. I was hungry and could almost taste Kimberley's breakfast. Sliced oranges, pineapple, kiwi, I imagined.

I invented a scene. A photographer with a long camera. Kimberley, in a bikini, lifts her chin and strikes a ballet pose. Her skin gives off gold. Her new friend, the model she met on the plane, fixes her eyes on Kimberley and watches from a distance. The photographer raises a hoop covered with a sheet to give off more light. Kimberley runs in and out of the ocean, tossing her hair this way and that, laughing as she hugs herself. The photographer crouching, bending, *click click click*, shooting his roll of film. Then, dropping tripod and camera equipment on the sand, they all fling CLUB MED towels across their shoulders, taking a break, as they run through pale dunes.

I carried the fantasy further. Surf spray washes their toes as they wade in waves. Kimberley stoops to pick up a few conch shells. Is one for me? No, she gives some to the photographer and the rest to the model. Suddenly, everything fades and what I see miles away is a lovely young girl who looks lost.

The sandpiper had followed me up and down Menemsha's beach. I searched for my footprints but they were no longer there. The tide washed them away. I took it as an omen. Something bad was going to happen. Furious with my mother, I kicked clumps of wet seaweed at the sandpiper who was still hop-hop-hopping beside me. "Leave me alone!" I said to the sandpiper. Or was it to my mother?

Dear Maggie,

I wish summer could go on forever. Everything's better in the summer. I dread school and all those awful tests and scores. I'm scared I'll never get into college. I'm not sure I'm good enough. Maybe I'm not the right material. I won't think about it now. Ziggy is great! He makes me feel important and not just because my parents are rich with champane and horses. He says I've got more than I know and he doesn't mean pounds Ha Ha. I feel like Somebody when I'm with him. Then I remember school and the low persentile I'm in and the feeling goes away. I wish I was skinny and beautiful and smart like Kimberley. Then nothing else would matter. She's so lucky. I'll always be grateful to Ziggy for seeing something in me that no one else did. I just wish I could feel like Somebody for longer periods then when Ziggy, Midnight and me are together in the stable.

xxxx yoyo 😊

P.S.   Remember the last night of camp when we wished on a candle and sent it across the lake?
P.P.S.   What would you wish for now?

# ELEVEN

The weather turned cool the week Kimberley was in Eleuthera. Extra blankets. Sweaters and sweatshirts. Logs in the fireplace. Too soon, my father would be locking up the cottage. My mother would slip the key under the mat. Jenny would fall asleep on the car ride back home. Eloise would throw up. And I'd shut my eyes and pretend that the summer was just beginning.

Snow decided to leave the Vineyard early to attend a meeting of the Goldfish Society of America. Clipper stayed behind to help with the outdoor furniture. Toby changed her reservation because she needed to see her dermatologist. Bimbo went home with Toby so he could have his guitar fixed in a music store on Forty-second Street. Zach was spending a lot of time in the library. I had no idea where Munson was.

The phone kept ringing. My summer friends.

"I'll see you . . . are you there, Maggie?"

"Yes, I'm here."

"There's static on the line."

"Bad connection."

"Don't forget, we'll get together over Thanksgiving vacation."

Forget? As if that were possible.

"Circle it in your date book."

"I already did."

The Who Cares — each one holding on, needing to be linked to that perfect summer.

Then, unexpectedly, it was Zach. "Hi! What's happening?"

"Nothing much." Why was he calling me?

"How about meeting me?"

"I promised my mother I'd clean out the refrigerator."

"I'm only four minutes away from you, right here at the post office in Menemsha. C'mon!"

"Well . . ." I thought of the milk that had turned sour, the bruised broccoli, the moldy lemon slices.

"I knew I could count on you, Maggie." He hung up quickly.

How could I refuse? I asked myself. Hadn't Kimberley wanted me to keep an eye on him?

I saw Zach before he noticed me and realized how handsome he was. That tingle in the back of my knees. I felt breathless, as if I were on a seesaw, caught in mid-air. My insides knocked around, my heart suddenly in the wrong place. His hair had grown shaggy and his beard needed trimming, so there was more red than usual. He wore a blue turtleneck and white jeans.

"You remind me of the American flag," I said.

"I'm bored." He offered me some candy.

"Calories." I shook my head. "Not everyone's a string of spaghetti, like you."

He threw back his head and laughed. The beard under his chin was a deeper shade, more like burgundy. "I really miss Kimberley," he said, looking down.

"She'll be back in a couple of days," I consoled him.

"And then?" he said as he waved to a mailman coming out of the post office. "I never know what to expect. Part of her with me, part of her God knows where, as if she were sawed in half by a magician."

I was shocked to hear him talk like that. Did he know something? What, exactly, was there to know? I felt I should defend my friend. But, for some reason, I said nothing.

He went on. "Or else she'll be so loving and sexy that I'll go crazy."

My stomach did a cartwheel. I glanced away. He seemed not to notice.

"Summer's already a memory," Zach said. I remember thinking that he sounded like Kimberley, that it was something she might have said. They were meant for each other. I never saw it any other way.

We began walking, silent for a while until he asked, "Penny?"

Should I tell him that I was wondering what I was doing there alone with him? That, without Kimberley, I wasn't sure we had enough to say to one another. Long gaps in conversation always made me nervous.

"Thinking of Kimberley?" he guessed.

I nodded.

"Sometimes separations are good."

I stared at him. "Never."

"You see yourself and others differently," he said.

I could listen to Zach forever. He was so mature, so wise. He never tried to impress anyone. He didn't need to prove himself. "Then why do you seem so lonely?" I asked.

"I miss her." He began walking faster. "It's really complicated." Faster and faster, adding, "I hate complications."

"Me too. I miss her, too." I almost had to run to keep up with him. "But I'm afraid of separations. I want everything to go on in the same way. I dread school. I don't want to leave the windmill. I don't want to be without you and Kimberley, Munson, the others —The Who Cares." I pictured all of us at a clambake on the beach and it made me sad. "I don't want to be without summer," I started to say but I knew that saying that would make me more unhappy.

"Well, Miss Me-too," slowing down until he stood still. "There are some things that have to end." He stretched out his long arm and rumpled my hair.

"You mean death?" catching up with him. "Like my grandmother?"

"Among other things."

"Like what?"

"Sometimes even — "

I interrupted before he had a chance to finish. "I hate endings."

"Endings follow beginnings," Zach said, adding softly, "In our beginning is our end."

Not another one of those quotes. "Shakespeare," I said, proud that I was finally getting the hang of it.

His hand rested on my shoulder. "T.S. Eliot," he

corrected. He was so tall that when I looked up at him I got a kink in my neck. If someone asked me to place an order for the perfect guy, I'd order Zach. A strand of linguine. *Al dente.* Just right. "I'm starving," he said, as if reading my mind. "Let's get something to eat."

We went into a nearby hamburger joint and sat perched on stools around a marble-topped table. The waitress brought a hamburger with french fries for Zach and a diet Pepsi for me. Zach asked if I'd mind changing seats. "I can't be near a mirror," he said.

"How come?"

"I've never been able to figure it out. It makes me uncomfortable. Something about my own reflection, I guess." He opened two packets of ketchup and told me a story about himself as a boy. There was a mirror that covered the length of the hallway in his apartment and whenever he passed it he had to turn his head the other way. Asking the waitress for more ketchup, he paused before going on. "I never told anyone that before," he confessed.

"Not even Kimberley?"

He shook his head.

That pleased me. "I think you should go into the mirror business," I said.

His hand moved to the back of my neck, just inside the collar. "You're a sweet one, Maggie Me-too," he said, pressing his fingertips on the place where there's a bone. What's it called? I should have remembered from biology.

"But it's true. You're awfully good-looking!" Talking to him was easier than I'd ever imagined.

He took his hand away and ate his hamburger. I

couldn't take my eyes off him. His legs were too long to fit under the table so he kept them crossed outside. I was careful to sit a certain way so that my jeans didn't brush against his.

At one point I reached for one of his french fries and heard myself say, "Watch out for Hollywood talent scouts!" I couldn't believe I had such nerve. I must have embarrassed him because he regarded me with a puzzled smile and changed the subject. "Kimberley and I came back here last winter," he said.

"What's it like off-season?"

"Isolated, with a foot of snow on the porches. Hardly anyone visits."

"Haunted houses?"

"The tide's down and the birds have gone south. We went ice skating. A bunch of us rented a wagon for a hayride and we sang Christmas carols."

Feeling left out, I said, "Hay makes me wheeze."

"I'll never forget Kimberley's voice Have you ever heard her sing?" Zach asked.

"Once." I remembered something about a blackbird. Bye, bye, blackbird.

Suddenly, Kimberley was there. My mind put her on a plane in Eleuthera and flew her back to the Vineyard so that she was sitting on a stool between us. She was laughing, teasing Zach about something or other. He looked at her in a special way. I wanted him to look at me in that same way. Zach . . . Zach . . . I could almost hear her. Zach . . . Zach . . . Kimberley's tone kept him for herself, reminding me that he was hers.

I didn't want her with me. With us. Not even crawling around inside my head. I knew it was wrong, terribly wrong. But I couldn't help thinking it.

"Why do we talk about Kimberley all the time?" I dared ask.

"She's part of us," Zach said.

"Why did you call me?"

"Why did you come?"

Turning away from the table, I looked out the window at a sandy lane that led toward dunes. "You asked me to," I said, glancing back at his lean face.

"You had a choice. You could have cleaned out the refrigerator."

Zach was right. How could I explain when I, myself, didn't understand? "Kimberley has everything anyone could wish for," I said. "Sometimes I wonder what it would be like to be her." I was making a fool of myself and waited for him to make fun of me.

Instead, he stared at me with curiosity and said nothing.

"I used to feel that I was nobody. Then this summer happened. Kimberley happened. She's perfect." Anyone else would have asked me what in the world I was talking about. But somehow, don't ask me how, I knew that with Zach, no more words were necessary. Maybe I could go further and say anything, anything at all. I almost told him my dream. Last night I'd awakened still locked in the filthy cellar. The door was bolted. The window fastened. Why was I down there? What had I done? Go to your room, bad girl! Go to your room, naughty girl! But my room was upstairs, upstairs where I slept in the dormitory bedroom of our rented summer cottage. Only the windmill and the salt smell of the

ocean convinced me that the cellar was not my room.
A dream, a bad dream that I wished would go away.

"Where do fireflies go in the daytime?" Zach asked
me out of the blue.

"I don't know. Where do they go?"

"I haven't the faintest idea," he replied, grinning.

But I was certain that Zach, like Kimberley, had
brilliant answers for everything. "Of course you know!"
I accused, tearing off a corner of my napkin, which I
rolled into a spitball to throw at him.

"Well." He pretended to give it deep thought. "I hear
they hide on a shady leaf." Tossing a spitball back at
me, he added, "But that's not the point. Why do you
need to look up to everyone? You're you. It's more than
enough."

What did he mean? I wondered. Then I did something I shouldn't have. Still sitting so close to him, I
leaned forward, saying, "Can we see one another back
home?" And once again, "Can we?"

He frowned, dropping his eyelids. He was angry.
He had every right. I felt as if I'd opened a door without
knocking. It made me dizzy to be near him. I could
have parted the hair of his beard with a single breath.
"Why do you want to see me?" he asked.

I backed down. "Forget it," I said.

Suddenly, Zach questioned me. What sort of a childhood had I had? What were my parents like?

I told him how I wheezed when I was born, that the
vaporizer was always plugged in. Was he really interested? I went on about other allergies, describing my
mother rubbing some smelly cream from a blue jar on

bleeding spots between my fingers as my father read fairy tales aloud to me.

"Happily ever after," he remarked. "I never read fairy tales."

I wanted to touch him. "It's not too late."

Neither of us said anything for a while. What was he thinking? I wondered what it would be like to hear him say, "I love you."

At that moment, I realized I couldn't remember anything about Kimberley. I panicked, as if I'd lost her. "Please," I began, not sure of what I was going to say.

"Goddammit!" Zach said, knocking a spoon off the marble-topped table.

"My sister, Jenny, used to say, 'Gofferdammit!' when she was only four." I bent down to pick it up for him.

He reached for me, framing my face in his large hands as he whispered, "Something's going on."

What could I say?

"I must be out of my mind." His eyes avoided mine and went to a grilled-cheese sandwich at the next table.

And me? What about me? Did I honestly believe that I could come between Kimberley and Zach? What kind of a person was I? I had no business being there alone with him. "What are you talking about?" I said, as if I didn't understand.

"Don't ask me what I'm talking about," he said sharply. "No games. Not with me, Maggie." Maggie. No one had ever said it that way before. What did he see as he stared at me? Brown hair, blue eyes, a regular nose, and a mouth. Jeans, a tee, and sneakers. A teenager — sometimes smiling, sometimes holding back

tears. Often confused, temper tantrums over my hair,
saying yes when I meant no, storming around when I
wanted to be held, hating Jenny because she was everyone's little princess, once even spanking Eloise because
I was snubbed by a friend. Part child — Mommy, do
you love me best? Daddy, am I still your little girl? Part
woman — afraid of doing the wrong thing, tempted at
times to do exactly that, the wrong thing.

Maybe he thought I was pretty.

Now was the time to leave. A fantasy. That's all it
was. There was nothing between Zach and me.

Yet, gazing at him, I was filled with longing. I envied
Kimberley beyond words. I envied her so much that I
willed myself into being her. I borrowed her, if that's
possible. I borrowed her as easily as she'd borrowed
my sweatshirt and beach bag for Club Med. I felt,
finally, as if I were the person I wished to be. I was in
Kimberley's skin. Her hair, her eyes, her teeth, her
body, were mine. I became that other person.

And then I did an outrageous thing. I leaned across
the table to kiss Zach. What was I doing? A kiss, a
brief kiss. That's all it was. Did he kiss me back? I'm
not sure. I'd like to think that he did. Perhaps I only
imagined it. And yet, even now, I taste him on my
lips and wish that he might have kissed me again, kissed
me once more. Who was this terrible girl who waited
for Zach to say her name? Who was this terrible girl
who wanted still another kiss, a long, unforgettable kiss?
What then?

Go to the cellar, bad girl! Go to the cellar, naughty
girl!

Out of nowhere, I heard someone up front asking

the cashier for M & M's. "Every single box, I'll buy the whole batch!" he shouted.

"Oh, God!" ashamed to face Munson. How could he like me if he didn't know me?

Zach seemed amused, poised as ever, calling out to Munson, who came over. "What in the world are you two doing here?"

"I . . . I . . . we . . . that is . . ." I couldn't find the words.

Zach saved me. "I asked Maggie to meet me." The truth. How simple he made it sound.

"C'mon, Maggie." Munson pulled me off the stool. Together we went to the counter. The cashier was stuffing M & M's into a shopping bag. Now, I'd climb on Munson's bike. He'd suggest going to our rock but I wasn't in the mood. I glanced over my shoulder at Zach who chuckled to himself, muttering, "Gofferdam-mit!" as he got up and left.

If I could do it all over again, I'd never allow that moment that would later change my life. Perhaps, in time, I might forget what I'd felt for a boy who looked like the American flag.


When I got home my mother said that Mrs. Porter, Kimberley's mother, had phoned and wanted me to call her back.

Something awful! I just knew it! I saw Kimberley's body . . . dragged from the ocean . . . her ankle bitten off by a shark . . . dangling from the wheels of a jet . . . splayed on the runway of the airport. . . . I couldn't help myself. The fears . . .

"Hello." Was it Kimberley's mother who answered?

"Hello, this is Maggie Gray."

"Yes, dear," she said. "I hope I didn't worry you."

"No," about to faint. "Is everything all right?"

"Yes, of course," she said. "Everything's fine. It's just that Kimberley asked me to tell you that she won't be home on schedule. The weather delayed shooting . . . only a few more days."

"Oh." Why didn't Kimberley call *me?* I wondered.

"She tried reaching you," Mrs. Porter said, "but the lines were down."

"Oh, thank you. Thanks a lot."

"I'm glad Kimberley has you, Maggie. You're good for her."

What a strange thing to say, I thought, not knowing how to reply.

"I hope we meet soon," Mrs. Porter said.

"Yes," I said. "Me too. Good-bye." That was Angela! She sounded sweet. Considerate. An angel. An angel with wings. Not at all the way Kimberley described her.


"Now, will you *please* clean out the refrigerator?" I heard my mother say.

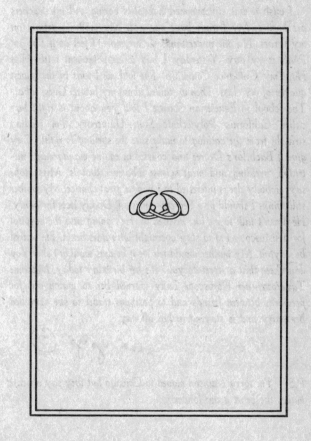

*Dear Maggie,*

*I wish it was still summer! School is boring. All my teachers are boring. My friends have changed. My mother's getting on my nerves. No one understands me anymore. I feel as if I've got PMS every day. Yesterday I had an appointment with Miss Hope my Guidance Councillor. She told me I was in the lowest quarter of my class. Then we talked about my future. Guess what? The school in Equestrian Sciense I told you about is right here called California Polytechnic State University. I'm reading straight from the catalog to make sure the spelling is right. They give a Bachelor's Degree and courses in equine management, nutrition, breeding and meat sciense whatever that is. Miss Hope says nobody else is interested so I have a great chance! My mother still thinks I should be a Secretary instead. Daddy acts far away. He doesn't talk to me like he used to. He's going into the hospitol for a sistoscopy (?) to stay overnight with anesthezia. I'm scared he's dying. My mother would tell me if he was wouldn't she? You don't keep that a secret do you? It's her birthday today. Madame Tavorozzi her Horoscope Lady warned her to watch out for fireworks between freinds and to postpone travel so she cancelled her party and is staying in bed all day.*

xxxx yoyo ☺

*P.S.   I'm sorry Munson moved to Chicago but they say absense makes the heart grow fonder.*

# *TWELVE*

*F*inally, at the end of September, Kimberley kept her word and invited me for a sleepover.

"What will I wear?" I asked her when she phoned. "What should I bring? What will we do?" I'd carried Kimberley around with me into autumn. We labeled colored folders for class, she waited for me at the allergist, we bought new Reeboks, and when I tried on clothes, she told me which jeans were too tight. My mind never let her go.

"I've missed you." She spoke softly into the receiver.

"Me too."

"How's school?"

"Boring," I said. Then, "How's Zach?" It wasn't easy for me to mention his name.

With a laugh, "Not boring."

Kimberley! Only Kimberley! I thought as we made plans for my trip to New York.

That first week back home, I'd met my old friends

at the stationery store for school supplies. They asked me the same questions. "How was your summer?" "Anything new at the Vineyard?" "Catch any fish in the harbor?" "Any good movies?"

Were they so wrapped up in themselves that they never noticed how different I was? A new habit of twisting a strand of hair around my finger? Opening my eyes wide as if I saw something no one else did? Walking a certain way?

I had no reply as we went past reams of typing paper and speckled notebooks. Why didn't I describe Munson's curls? Or Zach's red beard? And what about Kimberley? Why was I so silent? After all, we'd shared everything since first grade. They'd be fascinated in the same way I was. . . . Why so guarded? Looking around for paper clips and Magic Markers. Was I afraid that one of them might take Kimberley away from me?

I felt guilty. "There's a girl — " I began.

"Girl!" Shrieks of laughter across Hallmark greeting cards. "Who needs another girl. How about boys? Got any of those, Maggie?" with sarcasm, so certain that the very idea — at least for me — was impossible.

And a boy named Munson, I thought. What stopped me from saying his name aloud? Didn't I trust them anymore? Were my old friends already a part of my past? Why was everything changing so quickly? "We seem to be losing one another," I nearly said. But they would have looked the other way in embarrassment.

Little Neck . . . Bayside . . . the train to New York was moving too slowly. At last, the conductor called out, "Pennsylvania Station!" Carrying my suitcase, I

took the escalator and crossed the street to hail a taxi.
"Take a cab," Kimberley had said. "It's the fastest. I'll
pay you back."

I pressed the buzzer. "It's me," I said, when she
opened the door.

Laughing, she blew kisses and spun around in wide,
loose trousers and a huge, double-pocket silk shirt. She
moved in and out of poses, eyes flashing, throwing back
her head, twisting, turning, freezing, as if obeying in-
structions from a photographer who zoomed in with a
camera. Smile. *Click.* One more smile. Relax.

I remember wishing that we were back on the beach.

"What's wrong, Maggie?"

"Nothing."

She explained that she'd just come back from another
fashion shoot. "A portrait ad," she said. "One of those
angle shots without props." She smoothed her lip gloss
with a pinkie as she glanced at herself in the hallway
mirror and then hung up my coat.

If only I could look like that in pants!

"It's tedious work for easy bucks," Kimberley said.
"Angela once asked me what I'd do if she were no longer
around."

Angela. Once again . . . Angela. Why not Mother?
My mother? Mom? Even Mommy? It sounded, somehow, as if they never touched, never even kissed good
night. It puzzled me. She was so warm over the telephone.

"Angela says you should always work because you
never know when you might have to stand on your
own two feet." Kimberley sighed. "She keeps reminding
me of what happened to her after Daddy died."

"What happened?" Was there something I'd forgotten?

"You know, I told you. We were rich and then we were poor."

"Oh, yes . . . that."

"So, I decided I'd better get a job. I went to a modeling agency and they hired me part-time after school. The money made Angela happy. She adores money." Kimberley dropped her voice, saying, "I was nervous about seeing you, scared that things might be different between us."

"That's impossible." It was something I feared, but it never occurred to me that Kimberley might also.

"Anything's possible." Those pale green eyes were suddenly too intense for me. She reached for my hand and pulled me toward the living room. How often I'd fantasized about her apartment, even drawing pictures of it in my head.

"What, exactly, did you expect?" Kimberley asked, an amused expression on her face.

"I'm not sure."

"Knowing you, Maggie, you'd certainly have imagined something."

I guess I thought it would be special in the same way that Kimberley was. Dramatic, wild colors, personal touches here and there. But it was drab and cold. A hotel lobby. A couch, two chairs, a coffee table, TV.

"Well?" I heard Kimberley once again.

I was dumbfounded. What could I possibly say? Where was Theo, Kimberley's father? I was sure that on a table there would be a silver-framed photograph of the man she always spoke of: black wavy hair, dark

eyes, and a pearl stickpin in his tie. I looked around
for snapshots of him. Standing with Kimberley under
a tree in Central Park. Another, taken earlier in his
lifetime, holding Kimberley as a baby. And one more
of the two of them smiling into the camera dressed up
for their Sunday walk. It makes no sense but I wanted
to meet him, smell his Bay Rum after-shave that Kimberley often described.

"Well?" This time Kimberley was impatient.

"I thought it would be different," I confessed.

"You're such a romantic, Maggie," she said, somewhat
annoyed. "I told you Daddy died at the wrong time,
that business was lousy because of imports." She paused
for a minute before saying, "Angela never forgave him
for dropping dead and leaving her with all his debts.
She needed cash so badly that she had to sell his Tiffany
watch and gold cuff links, even some etchings."

I imagined Angela in rags.

"After that, Angela didn't seem to care about anything. She took a lot of pills, still does." Kimberley
went ahead of me toward the dark living room. "Now,
she has Dr. Multz, a famous plastic surgeon. Very rich
and very dull." Her smile was wistful as she plopped
on the couch, looking so small inside voluminous trousers and shirt.

I sat next to her and found myself wanting to yank
her off the couch and put her in the hot sun on the
beach where she belonged.

She picked up a carved wooden Buddha from the
coffee table and, holding it against her heart, she began
to speak of her father, always her father. "Daddy gave
me this," she said, as if dreaming aloud. Her voice curled

around the word, Daddy. I tried to do the same. Daddy,
I said to myself and thought of my own father. I made
believe he was dead just to see what it felt like. But I
couldn't even pretend. The pain was too unbearable! I
didn't say how frightening it must have been for Kimberley to have lost her father when she was only eleven.

"My happy Buddha," she went on. "Daddy told me
to rub his belly for good luck." She seemed about to
cry, her mouth tightly clamped. "I guess it doesn't always work," she said. Then she placed the Buddha back
on the coffee table. "I miss him, Maggie. If only Angela
hadn't lied to me when he died. Now, I'm always
lonely."

Always lonely? I thought. But what about Zach? Why
didn't she mention him? Did it have anything to do
with me? I hadn't said a word about our afternoon
together. If he spoke of it at all, how would he describe
it? How would I?

"Please don't be lonely." I touched her. "You have
me."

"Yes. Yes, I do!" Kimberley said, almost too brightly.
Then she led me into her room.

By that time, I should have known better. I'd expected ribbons and lace, white wicker, a canopy bed,
ruffled pillows. Somewhere, old-fashioned dolls. It was
all in shades of brown. How I hated brown! Brown was
a wooden coffin. Brown was dirt thrown over my grandmother's grave. Brown was the stem of a flower dropped
at the cemetery. It was a sad-colored room. I almost
started to cry. I'd grown to love Kimberley so much.

"Take that look off your face!" she said. "I suppose I
could liven it up. Do something quirky like tack love

notes on the ceiling." She raised her head. I could almost see Zach's letters in a thin column above us. "But who gives a damn?" she said. "I don't intend on staying here forever."

I wasn't sure what she meant, so I just shrugged.

Her room was a mess. Bobby pins all over, spilled Chanel dusting powder, paperbacks piled high on a chair, her portfolio stuffed with 8 × 12 glossies, pocketbooks hanging from doorknobs, Clinique jars and hair spray lined up on the floor, bottles and prescription vials everywhere.

"Clutter makes me happy!" she said, wiggling out of her trousers and shirt into jeans and a yellow sweater. "I slip the day worker an extra ten *not* to tidy up!"

We got the giggles. I'd almost forgotten how much fun we had when we were together. Kimberley could be silly about anything, even her dreary apartment. I wanted summer to return. But I couldn't have it my way. It was autumn, and Kimberley was saying, "When I wake up in the morning and see this hodgepodge, I know I'm really here."

I could hardly breathe when she said things like that.

Suddenly, a clinking noise like an automatic ice-maker.

"Angela!" whispered Kimberley.

Drifting into the room, first an armful of gold bracelets with dangling coins, then a woman with black hair wearing a black dress. "There you are," she said to Kimberley. Seeing me, she smiled. "Hello, Maggie."

"How do you do," I said in a polite voice, the voice of a girl who made her parents proud.

"Exhausted," she sighed. "I had to redo the windows

facing Madison, dress the mannequins in winter wool, and my back is killing me. I'm going to have a lie-down." She slowly reached out her hand toward Kimberley. "Don't forget, Dr. Multz is coming for cocktails. You won't mind saying hello?" She whirled around to leave.

"She's attractive," I commented. I was afraid to say that I thought she was beautiful because I knew it would make Kimberley angry.

"She works at it," Kimberley snapped, as I knew she would.

Then, sitting cross-legged on the floor, we talked about how much we missed Martha's Vineyard and how hard it was to be home. Why wasn't it the same with old friends? Whose fault was it? Theirs? Ours?

"Munson's unhappy in Chicago. He writes twice a week," I told her.

"Yes?" she said vaguely. "What?"

I almost reached into my bag to read her one of Munson's letters.

*Dear Maggie,*

*I miss you. Chicago is cold. School stinks. The guys are jocks. The girls are ugly. Please send me a picture of you. Do you remember our rock? I do.*

*Love, Munson.*

But I decided not to. She didn't seem to care.

When was she going to say something about Zach? Once again, I waited for his name. I was wondering if I should bring it up first when I heard her say, "I love fall, the leaves dropping."

"Autumn makes my mother sad," I said.

"Angela goes straight for the pills."

"Maybe she misses your father as much as you do." I couldn't help it. Part of me felt sorry for her.

Kimberley stared.

"You'll never forgive her?"

"Never! Angela's into Angela," Kimberley said sharply. "She never notices me." Kimberley got up off the floor and began to dance. *Plié. Relévé.* She'd taught me the steps over the summer. "My grades are down," she confessed.

"A-minus?" I kidded around.

"I got a B on a paper. Someone else got an A-plus and the teacher read hers to the class."

She couldn't be serious. Why was one grade that important?

Kimberley balanced an *arabesque. Pas de deux. Promenade.* "Everyone expects me to get A's," she said. "I never used to mind the pressure but now I'm scared. Suppose they see through me and think I'm nothing?"

I sensed something like terror, a look in her eyes. "Nothing!" I said. "But you're everything!" I flashed back to the first time we met. "You even speak Italian!"

"Italian?" Now she was doing stretch exercises, hands reaching for the ceiling.

"That day we had lunch at Giovanni's." I reminded her. "You spoke Italian to the waiter."

Legs apart, in perfect shape, palms flat on the floor, she lifted her head and said, "I was nervous, showing off to impress you."

I stood up and watched her. "Me?" And all this time

I worried that *I* never measured up and wondered what I could offer Kimberley.

"YoYo never stopped talking about you!" Kimberley kept pushing her hair back with both hands. "I memorized the words off a tin of macaroons from an Italian restaurant." She smiled, leaned forward. "Vinnie, the waiter, knows me, goes along with anything."

I laughed, saying, "Macaroons!" Isn't she something! I thought.

"I'm so down," she said, her thin body suddenly still. "So tired. I can't sleep. Yesterday, I stayed in bed all day."

"Sometimes I'm down, too," I said. Then I forced myself to ask about Zach. Was it my imagination or did she stiffen?

"Zach seems different," she admitted.

"Different? How? What does he do? What does he say?" I pressed for details.

"Something's not quite right. There's less of him. He's not really with me. It's hard to explain. . . ." She was pacing, breathless, a little scattered. "As if one key of a piano was slightly off."

I felt Zach's lips. Hardly aware of what I was doing, I rubbed my cheek as if his red beard had scratched it. Sssh! Behave. I warned my heart. "Zach will always love you," I said to Kimberley. I believed it. I honestly did.

"No one understands," she said. "No one."

"But I do!"

"No, Maggie. Not even you."

Perhaps she was right. Yet, I was surprised to see her go to her dresser and open a drawer, pulling out the

silver pillbox and brown bottle. "What are you doing?"
I was frantic at her dark mood.

Carefully, she opened the pillbox.

"Not aspirin?" I asked. The answer was obvious.

"Never aspirin," in almost a whisper.

"All those times?"

"Uppers to pep me up. Later, Valium. I filched Valium
from Angela. Once, I tried coke, only once."

"And the brown bottle? Not apple juice?"

"Wine, cheap Gallo. I decided against champagne.
Taittinger Brut or Moët Chandon would have been *de
trop*, don't you agree?" She was turning flip, her way, I
knew, of dealing with fear. "Don't you *dare* tell!" she
said. "You gave me your word! Your promise!"

As though I could forget. As though I could ever
forget. "I had no idea, Kimberley, not really." Then I
begged her to get rid of everything. "We'll do it together," I said. "Now! Please!"

"It's too late." She gulped several pills. "Everything
hurts me," she said. "My head, my stomach, even a pain
in my lower back."

Why didn't I grab the pillbox and bottle and throw
it all out the window. Why? I've asked myself a million
times. Would everything have been different? Was it
up to me to take charge? Should I have told someone
about Kimberley? If I broke my promise, I'd lose her.
How would I take that risk?

"You're furious?" she asked in a tiny voice.

How could I be when I felt the way I did? Later,
much later, I'd learn that I was, indeed, angry, very,
very angry. But I would have denied it at the time and
so I said, "I'll never tell! Trust me!"

Within minutes, she began to change. She was Kimberley once again. The way I loved her. She'd come back to me, in one of her happier moods, as she made plans for the following day. "Tomorrow, we'll walk up and down Columbus Avenue stuffing ourselves on hamburgers and scallops and exotic cheeses. We'll buy a tie for your father at Charivari's, pickled wild cherries for your mother from the Silver Palate, a stuffed rhinoceros at the Petit Loup for Jenny." She paused, squeezing my arm. "Then, we'll cross over to Park for doggie bubble bath for Eloise."

I could almost hear the surf, almost feel the wind blowing the sand, for Kimberley looked exactly as she had at the beach, her skin giving off sunshine.

"Let's call YoYo," she said suddenly.

It never occurred to me to do anything other than what she suggested. "Okay, let's!" I said. "You have her private number?"

"Sure." She sat on her bed and put the telephone on her lap.

I sat next to her.

"It's ringing," she said to me. Then, "YoYo! Hi! It's Kimberley."

YoYo must have said "Hi!" also.

Then, "What are you doing?" Kimberley asked. "Baby-sitting for whom? Warren Beatty? Yesterday . . . what? Lunch with Bruce Willis and Demi?" After a moment, "Guess who's here with me? Maggie!" She handed the phone to me.

"Hi! No, we're not doing anything special. . . . I wish you were here, too. . . . But YoYo, we do miss you! Wait a minute, Kimberley wants to say something."

Kimberley grabbed the phone. "How's your father? . . . YoYo, I can't hear you. Of course we miss you as much as you miss us. Maybe more!" She covered the mouthpiece with her hand. "Here, you take it," she said to me.

I listened to YoYo. "Yes," I said. "You were right. Kimberley and I *are* great friends. . . . YoYo, why are you crying? . . . No, don't hang up! Please don't hang up."

Kimberley and I looked at one another. Her eyes filled. So did mine. I'd never cried with anyone before. I'd shared clothes, shampoo, combs, pencils, pens, books, records, school lockers, pickles, and candy bars, but never tears. I wasn't even sure why we were crying. For YoYo, who wanted to be with us? For Kimberley, who was hooked on pills? For myself, because of all the things that were happening to me?

Just then we heard, "KIMBERLEY!" Clinking, clinking, gold bracelets clinking in the air. Angela said, "Dr. Multz is here, Kimberley. He wants to tell you something."

Kimberley followed her into the living room.

When she was gone, I did something awful. I had no right but I went into the bathroom and snooped through the medicine cabinet. Why? What made me? What did I hope to find? Prescriptions filled the shelves. *One every 4-6 hours as needed for pain. Two before bedtime. One every four hours for nausea. One capsule 4 times a day. Three times a day before meals. Daily as needed.* The name ANGELA PORTER was typed on each label. Kimberley's mother! Who took more pills, I wondered, Kimberley or her mother? Terrified that I'd be found, I quickly closed the medicine cabinet and slipped into Kimberley's room.

Kimberley came back and said, "Guess what? Free facelifts. They're getting married. Dr. Multz is going to be my stepfather!" Her face crumpled. "Do I have to call him Daddy?" she sobbed.

It was a heartbreaking moment. How could I help her?

After a while, she said, "I almost forgot. You're invited to an engagement party. Beginning now."

"But I can't. I'd be in the way. I don't belong."

"Neither do I." Kimberley took my hand.

Dr. Multz had brown hair and a brown mustache. He wore a brown suit with brown shoes. *POP!* Opening a bottle of champagne, he gave us each a glass and toasted, "To my Angela."

Kimberley looked unsteady, as if pulled from the ocean's undertow. Then she struck a pose and smiled for the camera that wasn't there. I glanced at the glasses we held. Each one was a different color. They were like Christmas balls. The wine goblets! I remembered that day at the beach when Kimberley told me about her father and his wedding gift to her mother. "Never feel sorry for me," she'd said. "*Never!* Besides, someday I'll inherit the wine goblets."

I saw her pushing those eyes right through her mother and Dr. Multz. Then, head bowed, she said nothing. Were we thinking the same thing? That Theo, her dead father, was there with us? Black wavy hair, dark eyes, a pearl stickpin in his tie. . . . Could she smell his Bay Rum after-shave?

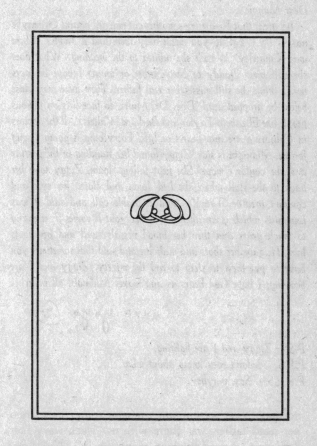

Dear Maggie,

It's great that Kimberley's mother got married again! Or maybe not. Is it? What do you mean only them and a Judge? Where was Kimberley? Wasn't she invited to the wedding? What does she call him? Daddy or Step-Father or what? I hope he loves her. I think she still misses her real father. They were very close before he dropped dead. Does Dr. Multz do face lifts on famous people like Elizabeth Taylor and Barbara Walters? All the doctors in California are into hearts or lifts. Everything is going wrong for me. Midnight is sick. Ziggy found her standing in the pasture and she couldn't move. She kept falling down. Ziggy took her back to the stall where she lied down and closed her eyes and couldn't breathe. The Vet paid a Stable call and said it was Laminitis which is an allergy just like you! It comes from eating to much grass and then her blood vessals swell and her hoofs hurt. He gave her shots and medicine and said that sometimes you have to put them to sleep to end the mizery. Ziggy and I are praying. I hope God hears us and makes Midnight all better.

xxxx yoyo ☺

P.S.   Ziggy and I are fighting.
P.P.S.   I don't even know about what.
P.P.P.S.   Sex, maybe.

# THIRTEEN

Then, suddenly, it was Thanksgiving vacation. The Who Cares. One night we were all at Kimberley's apartment. Her mother and stepfather were out. They were seldom home, always at dinner parties, she'd told me. I'd already imagined the beginning of the evening. Everything would be wonderful. Even her gloomy apartment would have changed. We'd laugh and crack jokes, summer sounds of us together again.

"I've missed you!" Munson grinned as he grabbed me. "What's different?" He studied me. "More grown-up, that's it."

"You're too skinny." Zach wrapped his long arms around Kimberley.

"Well, here we are!" Toby said with a smile, as Bimbo carried his guitar into the living room.

"School's a drag," said Snow.

Clipper gave a deep yawn.

"I've had a lousy three months," said Munson.

"Let's go back to summertime," remarked Zach.

Kimberley collapsed into a chair and closed her eyes. She wasn't going to disappear, was she? Go off on a journey somewhere inside her head. I expected Zach to bend down and whisper something to her. Instead, he leaned toward me and said, "Hello, Miss Me-too," as if we were alone, perched on stools around a marble-topped table. Kimberley's eyes were still shut. Had she heard?

I thought of last week when Kimberley had phoned. "Let's make a date. You and Munson, Zach and me. Just the four of us." She faltered a bit before saying, "I need you. Zach seems to be fading. He kind of drifts when we're alone." It was one of the weirdest conversations we've ever had.

"What's the matter?" I'd asked her. "You sound funny. Cold and distant."

"Distant?" she repeated.

"Flat."

"No," she replied. More flatness.

"Are you angry at anything?" At someone? Me?

"Should I be?" As if maybe she was, but didn't want to discuss it.

"But you sound so odd," I persisted, hugging the phone.

"My voice is my voice, my tone is my tone."

What did that mean? I wondered. "I feel you pushing me away," I said.

"So the problem is mine?" Icy.

"I didn't say that." I wanted to tell her to stop. My chest was tight. I'd become hoarse. Not another wheeze?

No longer talking about us, she went on, so softly that I thought we'd been disconnected. ". . . something's wrong, maybe there's someone else."

Could she hear my heart pound over the phone? Was she testing me? Doing this for my benefit? But there was nothing. Not really. Only a kiss in her absence. Or had I imagined it? Invented what I wished for? A kiss that probably Zach had forgotten? I tried to put him out of my mind. But sometimes he sprang up before me, tall as a tree, arms and legs like pick-up sticks, his beard still another shade of red, the color of an autumn apple. "There's no one else!" I said. "How could there be?" Then, after a moment, "Shouldn't we invite the others? The Who Cares?"

"No," Kimberley had replied. "No, I'm not up to it."

"But we talked about getting together. They might be hurt." I didn't want just Munson and me. KimberleyandZach.

"Oh, all right," she said. "But you make all the arrangements."

I promised that I would. It was the least I could do.

Kimberley, still in her chair, put her hand on Zach who sat on the floor. Munson was sprawled on the couch near me. Toby, Bimbo, and his guitar were leaning against the wall. Clipper and Snow sat across the room.

Kimberley asked Munson if he liked living with his father.

"You'd think we'd have more to talk about, two men," he said. "I can't get used to not being a family. Mom in New York, Dad and me in Chicago. If only they'd

get together again. Not that I'm lonely or anything.
. . . It's just that . . ." He didn't finish.

"Why do we expect happiness?" said Zach. "Always
looking for it."

"Finder's keepers?" said Kimberley.

Zach caught my eye. "Any ideas on happiness, Maggie?" he asked, glancing up at me.

A pause, as I tried to stop staring at the top of his
head, his legs stretched out on that awful brown carpet.

Snow's comment: "There was a time when I couldn't
wait for tomorrow."

"Cat got your tongue, Maggie?" Zach took me un-
awares.

All I wanted, at that moment, was for him to move
away from Kimberley. I watched them, and I saw that
everyone else was watching them, too.

"How can you talk about happiness?" Munson said
with a tone of anger. "What about AIDS?" He drew xxx's
on his jeans and then crossed them out.

"I used to think that older people were always the
first to die," Toby said.

Kimberley replied without expression, carefully,
"What's the point? To be or not to be . . ."

"Oh, for God's sake, Kimberley!" from Zach, before
I had a chance to shout, "Shakespeare!"

She hesitated and then said, "Of course I sometimes
think of death. Doesn't everyone?"

Snow got up and roamed around the room before
saying, "How about some action?"

"Like what?" I asked, relieved that we were onto
something else.

"We could check out the theaters, autograph books at Brentano's," said Kimberley.

"Look at the stars from the top of the Empire State Building," Clipper said.

"Go back in time at the South Street Seaport," said Zach.

Bimbo preferred torch singing at the Algonquin.

"Wave to the Statue of Liberty," said Toby.

We laughed, a little too self-consciously. There was tension in the air, odd glances. Even at that precise moment, Zach shot me one of his. Had Kimberley noticed? Or was I making it up?

Kimberley looked ethereal. I thought of my mother's painting. I saw the canvas. Kimberley seemed to be slipping away from me, one half of her face unlike the other. Her thin hand holding the blue wildflower. Petals falling. My mother had captured something that terrified me.

Our conversation kept going back to the summer.

"Have you seen . . . ?"

"Do you remember . . . ?"

"I'll never forget when . . ."

As if we needed to be back on the beach. All of us at a clambake.

"I'm going down, awfully depressed," said Kimberley.

"Me too!" I said, and wished I hadn't. Miss Me-too. Maggie Me-too. I waited for Zach to say something.

Bimbo began strumming his guitar, singing,

> "I can feel the love inside my own,
> Touch your need inside me. . . ."

"Oh, God, not that again!" snapped Toby.

Clipper said she was sleepy and looked as if she was going to nod off.

"No problem." Snow said he'd take her home.

Somehow, everyone seemed different. I felt as if I'd gone to the video store to rent a tape I'd been waiting for and, on playing it, discovered that it was the wrong one.

Clipper and Snow were already getting up.

"I think we ought to go, too, don't you think so?" Bimbo said to Toby.

"Yeah."

"Excuse me?" Kimberley looked at them as if she had no idea what they were talking about.

"I'm awfully glad we got together," Snow said. "Let's . . ." He couldn't figure out where to go from there.

"I'm sorry," said Clipper.

In the next moment, the four of them were gone.

Munson held out his arms as if asking me to dance. We pretended that there was music. I followed his lead. He'd grown taller so that his curls were now above my head. "Not bad, Maggie. Not bad," he said, just as he had when we were scooting in and out at the square dance. But nothing was the same. Was I the only one who sensed it?

Kimberley and Zach stood together. He pressed her against him. How many times have they made love? Maybe it happened only once. Maybe twice. To me, they were movie stars. A coming attraction for a love story filmed in and around Manhattan. I tripped over Munson's feet when I saw Kimberley grab a bottle of wine before leading Zach to her bedroom.

Munson, watching them, pulled me to the couch. His fingertips touched my neck, moving downward, his mouth hard, too hard, opening mine. He gave little gasps that sounded like hiccups, saying my name over and over, "Maggie, *hiccup*, Maggie, *hiccup*, Maggie, *hiccup*, Maggie, *hiccup*, Maggie . . ."

I pulled away.

He moved even closer to me.

"I can't! Please!" as I jumped off the couch.

"Why not?"

"I'm not ready."

Trying to be patient, Munson smoothed the cushion in an attempt to lure me back.

"I'm not ready for that!" I pointed to the couch.

With a deep sigh, he rolled his eyes and said, "Here we go again." Gently, he took my hand and guided me until I stretched out beside him.

"I need it to be special," I whispered. "Not here on a couch."

"Not here on a couch, not on the beach, not on the grass, not on a bike. Where then?"

I shrugged. "I'm only fifteen!"

He raised himself on his elbow to stare at me. "For heaven's sake, Maggie, you're nearly sixteen! Should we save it for your birthday?" his voice edged with sarcasm. "By the way, when is it?"

"My birthday is February second," I replied in all seriousness.

"Well, maybe you'll grow up over the holidays." Hanging over me, he said, "I'll save all my money, starve myself, stay home every night and watch TV, so that I can afford another trip back here for the occasion.

I'll even sing 'Happy Birthday' as we have sex!" He'd kicked off his sneakers, and his socks were rough against my ankles.

"Munson, please . . ." I noticed they were mismatched. One blue, one gray.

"It's supposed to happen by now," he went on. "I was faithful to you in Chicago. It's Thanksgiving now and where's my thanks?" rushing headlong, breathless. "The whole world is doing it, everybody, all the kids in my school, everybody except me."

I could hear my father as if he were there, sitting on a chair in Kimberley's living room, observing me. "Who are these everybodies, Maggie?" he would demand in a tone that suggested it was time I learned they weren't as important as I thought.

I was sore from Munson's body on mine. "I can't!" I said firmly, sounding more sure of myself than I actually was. I was getting tired of all the pressure. Maybe it was easier to give in. Do it once and for all. Get it over with. Then I wouldn't have to worry about it anymore. Nighttime fantasies, what would it be like. IT . . . part of me wistful, part of me afraid . . . IT. "I won't!" I said, surprised that I no longer cared about everyone else. Suddenly, at that moment, the everybodies had disappeared.

"Oh, grow up, stop being such a baby!" Munson looked defeated, as if he'd remained on the bench during a crucial basketball game, never given a chance to play. "Maybe you don't feel the same anymore."

"Yes, I do . . . that first time on our rock . . ."

He interrupted with, "It was better then."

He was right. "But why?" I asked, wanting to get up

off the couch, but then I'd have to climb over him and that would make matters worse.

He tried to kiss me as he said, "We were happier. I don't know why."

I heard Kimberley's door open, her footsteps on the way to the bathroom, water running.

Munson's arm tightened around me.

My own voice, "No! No!" rising to drown out the *snap snap* of a silver pillbox. "No!" so that I didn't have to listen for a gulp from that brown bottle. "No!" louder this time.

Munson lashed out. "Damn you, Maggie, you're nothing but a tease!"

"That's not true!" unable to move, as I counted the seconds until Kimberley returned to her room.

Was it possible? No, it couldn't be. That voice, his, Zach's, "I can't take it anymore. I need my space!" followed immediately by hers, "I thought . . ."

". . . Wrong. You thought wrong."

I couldn't believe my ears!

"What's going on?" Munson asked, lifting himself off me, but only for a minute.

"Did you hear what Zach said?" I asked him.

"No, what?"

"That word."

"What word?" He couldn't care less.

"Space!" I said.

He repeated it. "So?"

"Don't you remember?" my face close to his. "The night of the fire? The Ouija board?" Without waiting for his reply, I went on, "What do the fates have in store for me? *Space* was Zach's word."

"It was only a game."

"Yes," I reassured myself. "Only a game."

But was it? Maybe it was something more. I thought of Kimberley's word. *Glow*. Then the fire had started. An echo of all the other words. My own. Petal. My mother's portrait of Kimberley. Her face, splintered, soft pastels, stains of brown. The blue wildflower. Falling petals. Soon, an empty stem. Why was I so frightened? I felt as if I'd lost my way.

Munson knocked a cushion from the couch as he strained to get closer to me. "How long do you expect me to go on like this, Maggie? It's time you put out!"

"What about me? Why can't you understand my side?"

"All I ever think of is you. I don't have forever."

"It's still no." I shook my head.

"Goddamn! What the hell!" He leaped off the couch. "I don't need you. Chicago is full of girls. I can take my pick."

Suddenly, I felt completely alone. How long would it be before I'd forget the way we clung to one another and made promises we couldn't keep?

". . . Girls lining up for me!" Munson boasted before putting his sneakers back on.

"I'll miss you," I said, and thought how, in the beginning, it was perfect. Maybe now I was being punished. After all, didn't Zach still wander around locked inside my head? Yet, I called out, "Munson . . . Munson . . ." as if we were on our rock once again.

"Yes?" looking down at me.

"Friends?" I said, and couldn't believe that, within moments, no more someone, no more Munson.

Silence.

It wasn't fair! What had I done? I'd told him what I felt. But he didn't want to hear. It had to be his way! He'd forget me. "Just a kid with a wheeze," he'd tell his Chicago pals, if he happened to mention me at all.

Had I ever loved Munson? Is that what was wrong? "I'll miss you a lot," I said to him, as I thought to myself, say something. Please say something.

Silence.

Suddenly, I got angry. Who did he think he was? Smug, puffed up like a frog. I wanted to smash my fist against that stubborn, stony face. Jumping off the couch, I struck him on the chest. He caught my wrist, twisting my arm. "You know all those M & M's you gave me?" I cried out furiously. "I'm allergic to chocolate! I threw them in the garbage, every single one! I didn't have the heart to tell you because there were too many hurts in your life already."

We were interrupted by more words from Kimberley's bedroom. "I gotta get the hell out of here!" coming from Zach.

Munson and I were horrified as we waited for her reply.

Faraway, quavering, "I hurt all over," she said.

Nothing, absolutely nothing from Zach.

Kimberley's voice pleading, "Please! Don't walk out on me! Not now!"

Munson and I jumped apart as Zach came into the living room. He looked dazed.

Kimberley was on her way to the bathroom again, moaning, "I feel sick."

"What is it? What's wrong?" asked Munson.

Zach's eyes moved from us to a mirror that hung nearby. He gasped. One hand flew up to cover his face. Visibly upset, his features clamped shut. What did the mirror show? My mind went back to that afternoon we sat perched on stools around a marble-topped table. He'd asked to change seats, confiding that mirrors made him uncomfortable. I hadn't understood. It was hard for me to imagine anything about himself that Zach didn't like.

I went over to him and took his hand. I noticed, for the first time, a slight quiver in his cheek. "Zach . . ." I said softly, moving close to him, touching his beard. My head fell forward until it rested against him.

Kimberley came out of the bathroom. Noticing us, she stopped suddenly. What was it she saw then? She froze, saying nothing. She didn't have to. I'd betrayed her. That's what she believed. In those pale green eyes, I saw the stare of someone who no longer cared.

Why did I suddenly remember my dream, the dream I'd been having almost every night lately? What was I doing in that dark, dirty cellar? Why couldn't I open the window? Unlock the door? Who sent me down there? Who made me stay?

I ran toward Kimberley to hug her. I knew that she'd listen to what I had to say.

But she was still staring. "Don't touch me."

"It's not what you think," I said.

My hands dropped to my side. I felt chills as I had a vision of myself without Kimberley. I longed to run away from everyone, but mostly from myself. If only I could escape to the far end of whitened beaches. If only everything was as it used to be, not so long ago, when Kimberley and I would run along the sand. "It's not what you think!" But I wasn't sure if I was telling the truth. Must I now part with the memory of Zach's lips on mine? Must I now give back that kiss that never belonged to me?

Suddenly, I needed to be back home. Home with Dad's jazz, Mom's paintbrushes, Jenny's questions, even Eloise's seizures. There, at least, things stayed the same. Mom and Dad. I'd never called them that before. When had they stopped being Mommy and Daddy? What was happening to me? Once again, I felt so alone.

I began to shake. I was shaking so hard that I felt dizzy. "I've got to be with my family," I said.

"Yes, I suppose so." Kimberley looked at me as if I weren't there.

When had we all become strangers? Munson, slumped against a wall, hardly noticing. Zach, avoiding the mirror by gazing out the window at the sky-scrapers. Kimberley, walking away; walking away from me.

I tried to tell her that I'd always be her friend. But I was afraid.

Opening the door, I wanted to be gone, away from Kimberley.

On the train ride home, I rearranged everything in my head. I saw Kimberley, tanned legs, cutoff jeans, a man's button-down shirt, a thick pigtail that swung

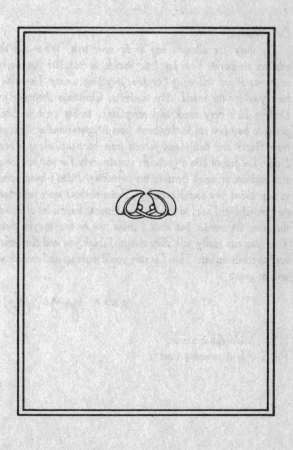

Dear Maggie,

   I'm sorry the allergist has to do more tests. When did the wheezes get worse? Your last letter sounds so cold. Are you angry with me? Please tell me if I've done anything wrong. I wouldn't hurt you for the world. My mother is Christmas shopping for Daddy. He's very weak and everythings to big on him. She's going to buy him red leather boots from Magnins and a silk scarf from Gucci and pants and jackets from bootiques along Rodeo Drive. I'm giving him a cashmere sweater only I'm not sure what size medium or small because hes shrinking. I don't know what to say about you and Kimberley. Theres nothing more important then freindship! I used to think it was better to have a lot of freinds the more the merrier but now I think one or two maybe three. Then you can really talk. Say things. I think you and Kimberley need to communikate. Then I'm sure you'll make up and everything will be great!

                                        xxxx yoyo ☺

P.S.    Midnight is worse.
P.P.S.    Is it snowing there?

# FOURTEEN

Christmas Eve, tomorrow Christmas. I could hardly wait! We were trimming the tree. It was crooked. It was crooked every year. Dad turned it around to hide the bare spots as Mom opened cartons filled with colored ornaments. Jenny and I argued about the tinsel. She placed each strand separately. I preferred throwing it in clumps. Packages with fluffy bows and Santa Claus gift tags were under the tree. Mistletoe hung from the ceiling. A cotton-stuffed unicorn with a gossamer mane and tail stretched out on the sofa. The scent of holly and balsam were at the front door. Jenny and I saved two tiny gold angels for last. She'd hang hers. Then I'd hang mine. I always made a wish, but I never told anyone what it was.

Snow was falling, whirled by the wind. I couldn't get Kimberley out of my head. Where was she? What was she doing? Her face was in every snowflake, smiling,

159

sad, sifting down from the clouds. Four weeks and one day and two hours and five minutes since that night at her apartment. I'd called several times but the phone was always busy. I was sure that she didn't want to speak with me. Was she still furious? Had she found another friend?

Suddenly, the phone rang.

Closing my eyes, I prayed as hard as I could, let it be her! Let it be her! Why should it mean so much to me? I wondered. I dashed upstairs where I could be alone. "Hello?" I said, crossing my fingers.

"Merry Christmas!" Kimberley sang out.

Nothing has changed, I told myself. We were as close as before. "Is it really you?" I asked.

She laughed, sounding more relaxed than she had in a long time. "Who else? Santa?"

"It's been lonely without you."

"At least, I know what to do now," she said.

"With what?"

"My life, obviously."

Hardly changing tones, she began to reminisce. "Remember the Vineyard? Why does it seem so far away?"

I flashed back to a sunny day at the beach when Kimberley was limbering up on the sand. She had squinted at me, smiling in a way that said she was happy, only she wasn't, was she? Suddenly, everything about that summer was beyond my understanding. The Who Cares — a club where wishes were granted and romance was certain. Or so I believed.

I nodded over the phone. "I remember," wanting to go further, but holding back, always holding back, wondering when her pain began. Did it start with Theo, her father who had died?

She sounded exhausted as she said, "What difference does it all make?"

But I clung to the memories. "Remember that rainy afternoon . . . Eloise . . . boo?"

"Poor Eloise."

". . . and the clambake when Bimbo stripped . . . ?"

"Things are falling apart," she said. "I lost a job doing catalogue work. . . . they want new faces. . . . a model from Australia . . ."

"She's ugly," I said.

"How do you know? You haven't even seen her."

"I just know. Next to you, she's ugly."

"Oh, Maggie, you *are* fun."

"So are you." See? We were having an ordinary conversation. It was all very comfortable. Soon, we'd talk about the weather.

"How come you're so normal?" she said.

"Normal?"

"It's a compliment," she said, adding, "Well, one thing's for sure. The pills . . . I took some."

What? I didn't quite catch it. Pills? Always pills. I hesitated, and then said, "I thought you were angry with me when you didn't call." Pills. More pills. If we don't talk about it, then it's not happening. She was being melodramatic. "What else is new?" I decided to make light of it. There was nothing unusual going on. Soon, we'd plan something for the next time we were together. She'd visit me and I'd show her the house. She was curious, always asking questions. When was the house built? Did we use the fireplace? Did we eat in the kitchen or the dining room? Had Jenny and I ever gone wading in the brook that ran along the back?

"There you go," I heard Kimberley say. "Safe in your never-never land."

There was music in the background. Was she at a party? No, it wasn't that kind of music. "Are you in your apartment?"

"Hmmm."

"Chopin?"

"Sonata #2 in B flat. I'm choreographing the scene . . ." She seemed to be humming, so carefree that she might have been holding the phone against one ear, examining the fingernails of her other hand, colorless nail polish accenting white half-moons.

It was getting creepy. Was there something I should have picked up? I searched in my head. Was it the time she . . . ? Or when . . . ? Why hadn't I paid more attention when she said she was low, real low? I'd seen it as moody, growing pains, something I'd felt so many times myself. "Where's Angela? Dr. Multz?" I wanted to know.

"Dancing at Roseland," she said. "Last week they won a prize for the tango."

"You're all alone?" I couldn't bear the thought of Kimberley without a family on the holidays. Without a Christmas tree, cards on the mantle, sprays of green throughout. An image of Angela would haunt me. Angela spinning, her gold bracelets clanking, twirling, in the arms of her new husband who wore brown.

"Yes, I'm all alone." I could picture her through

the telephone, shrugging her narrow shoulders.

"You have me," I reminded her. You have me. You have me. How often, I wondered, had I said those very words? You have me.

"Do I?" her voice rather cool. I knew that she was thinking of that night at her apartment.

How could she say, "Do I?" I guess she needed to hurt me. "Where's Zach?" I asked.

"He's gone, Maggie." Then she asked if I'd heard from him.

"Me? Why me?" That kiss. Had she known all along?

Kimberley began to say something and then stopped.

"Munson's gone, too," I said. Then quickly, "Zach will come back. He'll always love you!" Was I trying to convince her? Or myself?

"Never-never land again."

I began to babble. "I can never sleep the night before Christmas. It sounds childish, I know, but I still listen for the sound of Santa and his reindeer. Does that mean I don't want to grow up?" On and on, trying to take her mind off . . . off what?

"Guess what happened on the way to Christmas?" Kimberley sounded breathless, as if she'd gone ice-skating at Rockefeller Center, snow gathering on her eyelashes, sipping icicle straws as she hailed a taxi to go home.

"You were chosen Fairy Queen!" That was the way, the only way to get her out of it.

Thoughtfully, she said, "I saw a psychiatrist."

"Where? Shopping for pajamas at Bloomingdale's?" How clever I was! But I was already jealous of her psychiatrist. They'd have secrets. She would tell him things she never told me.

"It was only a consultation," she said without expression. "He prescribed some pills for my headaches."

"More pills?" Is that why she'd gone to him? Tricked him? I saw her silver pillbox. She would take the pills, one by one, between thumb and forefinger. Then, a gulp from that brown bottle.

In a tone of apology, "I wasn't completely honest with him, testing to see what it would be like . . . having a shrink." Finally, sounding flirtatious, "Obviously, I won't show up for my next appointment."

She couldn't be serious. She was too beautiful, too smart. She had everything going for her. And what about her date book, crammed with modeling appointments? *Vogue*? *Harper's Bazaar*? Another cover for *Seventeen*?

"I'm no one, not really," Kimberley was saying. "Hair up, down, pulled back, eyes open, closed, walk across the room, sit . . ." Almost everything she had ever done, she said, was to please others. "A pretty face for the photographer."

Was everything for the camera? That she was not what she seemed? That nothing was? Is that what she was saying? And me, what about me? Was I also not what I seemed?

"It's too late, much too late," slurring her words.

If only she was like everyone else! We all had rotten days. You slammed the door, collapsed on the bed, turned on the radio, and listened to songs about love. You washed your hair or spooned a pint of ice cream.

Kimberley got a kick out of livening things up. At the Vineyard, she'd worn rhinestone chandelier earrings with her jeans, or western boots and a bikini. Once, she drew black seams up the backs of her bare legs with an eyebrow pencil. Soon, she'd giggle into the receiver and say, "Lighten up, Maggie. I'm restless, bored, you know me!"

She began to hum again. "How can I tell if I've taken enough?"

I was numb as I imagined her sitting, huddled on her bed, bottles and vials everywhere. "You stupid jerk!" I shouted.

That struck her funny. She laughed, unable to stop.

"Kimberley, please . . . please," I said softly. I can't take this, I thought. Millions of girls have close friends. Why is mine doing this to me?

Should I tell her that I had to hang up, someone was ringing the doorbell, then call the police? Press 9-1-1. Wasn't there a special hot line? But what would I say? "Hello, this is Maggie Gray. I'd like to report someone who . . ." Then what? "She plays games, teases, takes a lot of pills . . ."

This isn't happening, I thought. But it was. "Kimberley," I said. "What about us?"

"Us?" in a flat voice. "What?" far away.

"I hate you!" I almost sobbed. Who did she think she was? An actress trying out for a part? An Academy Award performance, trembling voice, an intake of breath, all for effect, loving every single moment of attention. I'd never forgive her for putting me through this. Later, at another time, when she stopped moping around and apologized to me, I'd get even and be just as cool and distant as she could be.

Faintly, "Our little life is rounded with a sleep."

No, not that again. Oh, well, I'd go along. Anything was better than this. "Rip Van Winkle," I said. I thought that would break her up but it didn't.

"The Tempest," she corrected me, sounding somewhat drowsy.

"You and your snobby game of quotes!" I burst into tears. We were quiet for a while, so quiet that I wondered if the operator had disconnected us. I imagined telephone lines crossing the space between Kimberley and me. She was twisting a strand of hair around her finger, watching the snow cover Manhattan's rooftops.

"About being close friends . . ." she began. But she didn't finish. I had no idea what she was going to say. That it would never change? That it was all a mistake? Instead, she said, "When you were a little girl, what was your favorite game?"

"Dress up. Pretend," I said. "And yours?"

"Hide-and-seek." And then, her voice so near, as if her face were only inches away from mine, "I sent you a Christmas present."

I was touched, moved. What was it? A sweater? Cassette? Book? That's what I was thinking. But I never said it. Certainly, not aloud. But yes, that's what I thought. Me. Me. Me. Only me. "I don't have anything for you," I said. "Not yet. I wasn't sure if —"

" — It's over," Kimberley whispered. "No more."

What did she mean? No more of Maggie. I understood. Hurt, I shouted, "Damn those pills! Why didn't you stop?"

"I tried. Honest, I tried."

Suddenly, I heard no sound at all. Was she crying? I remembered those moments when her eyes unexpectedly spilled over. Maybe I wanted her to cry in the same way I was. Don't ruin Christmas. I beg you, don't! I almost said. Was I beginning to believe her? "Aren't you afraid?" I asked.

"Afraid?" She paused for a minute. "I've always been afraid. I thought you understood." Then she hung up.

Had Kimberley really gone? Left me that abruptly? No, she was still there, doing that funny thing with her hands, making a steeple with her fingers. She'd always be there. I was sure of it. If she'd done anything, I'd have felt her disappear.

But I was trembling as I called back.

Busy.

I tried again.

Still busy.

I could hardly breathe.

Busy.

Was the phone off the hook? Within moments, I began to wheeze.

Busy signal.

Soon, I'd need a Benadryl. "You'll be sorry," I muttered. Should I have the number verified? I put the phone back. I picked it up. Down. Up once more. This time I pressed 0.

"Operator."

"I'd like to report a busy line," I said. "Is it out of order or what?"

"What is the number you're calling, please?"

I told her.

"Just a minute. I'll try it for you."

Silence. No clicking. Nothing.

Finally, "That's a busy signal."

"Is someone talking?"

"Try it again. If it's still busy, you may call repair. Have a happy holiday."

I hung up, tried again. I listened and still it was busy.

Kimberley would call back. Christmas Eve, Christmas Day, my favorite time of the year. I needed it to continue. It must remain the same. Just as it always was. She knew what Christmas meant to me. She'd never spoil it. Or would she?

9-1-1. I pressed those numbers . . . 9-1-1 . . . and slammed the receiver before anyone answered.

On the way downstairs, I noticed my mother's painting of Kimberley propped against the wall. Something was wrong. Something hidden.

In the living room, Dad was checking the hooks for stockings. Jenny was counting the packages tagged with her name. Mom sat on the couch folding ribbons. Eloise was snoring, fast asleep in front of the fireplace.

I sensed Kimberley beside me, as if she'd lifted herself from the picture frame so that she could follow me. She was there, close to me, waiting.

There wasn't anything anyone could do. I reassured myself. Nothing was going to happen. Nothing bad could happen.

"Who was that? Who phoned?" My mother was curious in a way that she'd never been before.

Hang up call, I wanted to fib. But I said nothing.
Instead, I concentrated on the presents I'd bought with
money saved from baby-sitting. Jazz tapes for Dad. A
book from the Museum of Modern Art for Mom. Hoops
for Jenny's newly pierced ears. Doggie candy for Eloise.
This Christmas would be the best ever!

All my life I'd wished upon a star, skipped over cracks
in the pavement, walked around ladders, searched for
four-leaf clovers, hoping for happily ever after. Why
did I suddenly miss the little girl I was?

If only Kimberley would leave me alone. She seeped
into the outline of Christmas. Even as I gazed at the
ornaments on the tree, I felt something sad, belonging
to another time, another place. The wine goblets. The
colored balls hanging from the branches reminded me
of those wine goblets that someday would be hers.

My mother and I exchanged a look. Are you all right?
she asked without saying a word.

"Kimberley . . ." I almost swallowed the name, half-
hoping that my mother wouldn't hear, that I could take
it back if I chose. I still needed my happily ever after.
Without it, I'd have to be a grown-up and I wasn't sure
that I was ready. "Kimberley . . ." a little louder this
time.

"What?" my mother asked. "What is it?"

As if Kimberley prodded me, pushed me with her
thin hand, the hand that held the wildflower, I blurted
out, "She said she took a lot of pills."

I could feel Kimberley smiling at me with her eyes.
"It's about time, Maggie. What took you so long?" That's
what she'd say if she were really there.

An expression of horror on my mother's face as she turned to my father.

No longer hidden, "Is it too late?" I cried. "IS IT TOO LATE?"

A call to the police. The squash of down coats. Doors slamming. The noise of the motor. Tires churning. The rear bumper scraping a tree. Our car splashed snow on the way to New York.

Dad's shoulders tense as he hunched forward on the steering wheel. A strand of tinsel in Mom's frizzy hair. Jenny's small hand inside mine. Huddled together.

". . . sometimes, a cry for help . . ." from my mother.

". . . get a key from the superintendent . . ." from my father.

". . . careful, don't skid. . . ." Her.

". . . hospital, stomach pump. . . ." Him.

Dad switching on the radio. Mom turning it off. The windshield wiper sticking. A Greyhound bus on the parkway. A taxi whizz-banging. Freezing cold leaking through closed windows. The radio back on.

"REVISED FORECAST . . . SNOW CHANGING TO RAIN," the announcer was saying.

We'd been driving nearly two hours when the car braked to a stop.

I started to get out.

"No. Stay here with Jenny." Mom and Dad ran toward Kimberley's apartment building. Nearby, down the street, opposite the Museum of Natural History, a police car was parked.

The announcer went on, "ELECTION OFFICIAL INDICTED IN THEFT . . . NEW FINDINGS IN CRASH . . . SUBWAY KILLING . . ."

Jenny slowly reached for me as we sat in the backseat. "I'm scared, Maggie." Even in the dark, I could see tears on her face.

Kimberley would be answering the doorbell by now. She'd smile, delighted to see my parents. "Thank you for coming," she'd say in that too bright voice, as if nothing was wrong. Then Kimberley would introduce them to the police officers already there, charming everyone as she made believe her life would go on as before.

"BUSINESS BRISK ON BROADWAY . . . TICKETS AVAILABLE AT CARNEGIE HALL . . . MINUTES AWAY FROM THE RUSSIAN TEA ROOM . . ."

Teeth chattering, breath steaming, Jenny whispered, "Kimberley's not dead, is she?"

"I don't know." At another time, I'd have said something else, anything at all to reassure her, to take away the pain of growing up. "I don't know," I said again as I held her tight.

I prayed that soon we'd be home. Jenny would hang her tiny gold angel on the Christmas tree. Then I'd hang mine on the highest branch, the one closest to Heaven. I closed my eyes, shutting out the image of Kimberley buried in snow. Then I made my wish. I wished that Kimberley would be able to sleep over next year on Christmas Eve.

"DEPARTMENT STORE SALES 20 TO 50 PERCENT OFF . . . CALL YOUR TRAVEL AGENT . . . FLY AMERICAN AIRLINES . . ."

Jenny was pointing across the dashboard in the direction of the apartment building. "There's Mommy and Daddy!" She clapped her hands over her eyes.

They were hurrying to the car. An expression on
their faces made my heart beat terribly hard. Squeezed
together in the backseat, Dad clutched Jenny, and Mom
took me in her arms. "My darling," she said. "My darling," over and over again.

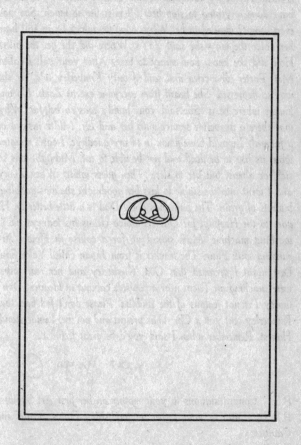

*Dear Maggie,*

*I wake up like nothing's happened. Then I remember. Kimberley is dead! Kimberley commited suicide! I can't believe it! Could we have done anything to stop her? I'll miss her so much. She was everything I wanted to be. Why, Maggie, why? I can still hear her voice the way she said YoYo. Where did she get the pills? How did she know how many to take? After your call I called Mrs. Porter who cried and said if only Kimberley told her she was so depressed. She heard from everyone except Zach. No one knows where he is. She said your family was so helpful. Why was there a graveside service with her and Dr. Multz instead of a funeral? I would have flown in to say goodbye. I can't imagine what its like to be dead and not be able to eat. Midnight was so sick we almost put her to sleep. Then guess what? When Ziggy and I went into the stable to kiss her goodnight she was gobbling buckets of grain. The pain was gone! Dad is a little better to. He goes to the Hospitol for Dialisis which cleans his kidneys like a washing machine. Mom signed up for a course in Flower Arranging with Flair. The teacher is from Japan called Yoko San. Last night I dreamed that God, Kimberley and her real father were snacking on Tacos near a poolside cabana in Heaven. Don't worry I'm not jealous of the Buddha. Please don't feel bad that Kimberley sent you a Christmas present and not me. I understand. Honest. Remember when I said you'd be great freinds!*

xxxx yo yo ☺

P.S.   *Congratulations to your mother on her first Art Show!*
P.P.S.   *Ditto to your father on publishing Ethics, Truth and Cavities.*
P.P.P.S.   *Ziggy is looking for another job.*

# FIFTEEN

"Maggie . . ." Dr. Woods says my name, soft as sand. Where am I? The foam of a wave. Low-tide beach. Gulls with open wings. A deserted dock. Icky seaweed. A sandpiper. "Maggie, would you like to read your sentence now?"

It's a while before I realize that Dr. Woods is calling on me. Once again I glance at the drawings by young children on the walls. Checkers, Sorry, dominoes stacked on shelves. Plants lined up on windowsills. Books on marriage, separation, divorce, death.

I begin. "What I like best about myself is . . ." I gasp and try to control a wheeze. "There's nothing, absolutely nothing that I . . ."

I can't say another word.

The girls in my group stare at me. They're waiting, still waiting.

I know I must continue and complete the sentence. Dr. Woods expects it. She's been so patient. I'm ter-

rified. "What I like best about myself is . . ." A rim of
pain around my throat. I can't breathe. "I hate myself."
I speak quickly, hardly recognizing my own voice. I
can no longer keep it inside. "I'm no good. If it hadn't
been for me, my friend, Kimberley, would still be alive.
She thought I tried to take Zach away from her, but I
didn't, not really. Part of me wanted to . . ." I let out
a little cry. "I should have broken my promise to her
long ago, told someone about the pills. But I wasn't
sure. I waited too long for everything."

There are deep sobs. Mine? It's unlike anything I've
ever done. "I'll never forgive myself. I feel as if *I* killed
her!" I look down at the floor. Who wants to see me
anyway? They're all thinking that I'm rotten, that I'm
a coward. They're right, of course. All my life I've run
away from anything I couldn't deal with. Now, I'm
getting what I deserve. Soon, everyone will leave me.
Not only Kimberley.

"I never knew anyone like her," I say softly. I share
a picture that comes to my mind. Kimberley is at the
beach staring out at the ocean. She sits cross-legged,
a blue vein trickling down the inside of her thigh. Her
skin tans the color of honey. The sun bleaches her hair.
Pushing those pale green eyes into mine, she is about
to say something. But what? No, she keeps it to herself
and breaks off a piece of rickety driftwood instead.

Something stops me. How can I admit that at this
very moment I'm not sure that Kimberley was real. Did
a wish place her so close to me last summer? Maybe I
made her up.

But I don't say those things.

"There's something else," I go on. "I'm angry, very,

very angry! She had no right to kill herself! Didn't she
think of me? Didn't I matter?" I stare at Dr. Woods and
wonder if she hears the rasping gurgle, the rattling
wheeze.

"It's all right to be angry," Dr. Woods says.

"But then I feel guilty."

Silence.

More spills out of me. "I have this dream . . ."

She leans forward, intent. "What kind of dream?"

"My cellar dream. I'm trapped down there . . ." I sit
motionless. I don't like being the center of attention.
Not in this way. My dream is my dream. I don't have
to tell anyone about it. Why do I? "Sometimes, I don't
believe Kimberley's really gone. I hold imaginary conversations." I shrug, as if embarrassed. "I catch myself
thinking of things to tell her, little things. I saw Toby
the other day . . . her skin's cleared up. She said that
Bimbo spends all his time at recording sessions. Clipper
and Snow broke up." A pause, tugging at my new
button-down shirt. I'd grabbed it off the rack because
it reminded me of Kimberley. Then, in a near-whisper,
"I should have known, I should have known."

"Known what?" Dr. Woods asks.

"What was happening." I can hardly swallow.

"You were fifteen, then sixteen," Dr. Woods replies.
"You loved her."

Is it that simple? I repeat it to myself. I was fifteen,
then sixteen. I loved her. But then why did I behave
as I did? Why did I kiss Zach when I knew it was
wrong? Why did I wait so long to tell my parents about
the pills?

I surprise myself by saying, "In my dream, I'm in the

cellar. I can't get out. I'm being punished." I remember — but had I really heard it? — the sound of the cellar door being bolted. The window fastened.

"Who is punishing you?" She presses for more.

I wonder, I thought, I wonder. I'm on guard, afraid of locking eyes with Dr. Woods. I speak without looking at her. "I never said good-bye." Drawing hard, stifled breaths, "I want Kimberley back with me so that I can say all the things I never did."

"Everyone has a cellar, a dark place to hide ugly thoughts."

I don't understand.

". . . a need, sometimes, to be something or someone else."

Over and over in memory, Zach's lips — losing myself in becoming Kimberley. That magical moment when I became the person I wished to be.

Is everyone laughing at me? Longing to be comforted, I almost lean my head against Dr. Woods. Instead, I blow my nose. "I can't stop crying," I confess.

"Tears are often valuable," she says softly.

Every part of me is trembling. "I don't know how to let her go!" Too restless to sit with the group, I move from window to window, past the drawings on the walls, past the games, the books, and think: Will I ever forget her?

A girl with unlaced sneakers gets up and puts an arm around me. I feel everyone watching. Before I know it, all the girls come over to me. Our hands touch. Then we walk back and sit down.

But now I'm out of control. "I was worried about breaking a confidence. I should have gotten help!" I don't mean to scream. "Is it my fault? IS IT MY FAULT THAT KIMBERLEY IS DEAD?"

Dr. Woods is speaking. I anticipate something terrible. I watch her lips. I see words leaving her mouth but I can't hear. Am I tuning out again? What is she saying? I must concentrate. "No," in a lowered voice, "it is not your fault. We all have choices. Kimberley was unhappy before she met you, way before."

I'm puzzled. There's something unexpected in her tone. I look for a scowl, mouth slanted downward. Her expression says she likes me. Is she crazy? After what I've done? What kind of a dumb psychologist is she anyway? Hasn't she had enough experience to realize how rotten I am? Why doesn't she scold me? Blame me?

"Kimberley must have felt very alone," Dr. Woods continues.

"She had me."

"And a cellar," she adds, "her own cellar."

Tears come into my eyes for my friend. In a way, it is the worst moment of all. She's not coming back. Kimberley is never coming back.

Dr. Woods goes on. "Kimberley's father gave her the Buddha. She sent it to you, Maggie, as a message of love."

I don't know what to say. Will she mind if I'm silent? I hear a door opening. A window unfastened. I'm running from the cellar. No one is keeping me there anymore. I wonder, I wonder.

"Your wheeze is gone," observes Dr. Woods. She seems pleased.

I sigh and wait for the familiar hoarseness. I take a

deep breath and still one more. Where is my wheeze? What has happened to my wheeze? Must I part with that, too?

Her smile is tender. Is it meant for me or someone else? "Perhaps next week when we meet," she says, "you'll be able to complete your sentence — what you like best about yourself."

Next week? Will I be able to move beyond now, or yesterday?

I glance at my watch. I just want to get out of there. I need to be by myself, alone with Kimberley whose portrait now hangs in my room. Near the door I pause, unable to stay, unable to go. I start to speak and fall silent. When will I be able to say good-bye? Will it always be a sad word for me? Colored brown? I'll try harder. "Good-bye," I say aloud on the way home. I say it to anything, to everything. To the sun, the trees, the supermarket, the Milky Way wrapper on the street.

I stop in front of my house and look for the wild-flowers. Those lovely blue wildflowers no longer growing on the front lawn. They're gone. They're dead. "Good-bye," I whisper to part of myself, that little girl who must have everything as it once was. "Good-bye . . . good-bye. . . ." I go on trying until the sound is right. "Good-bye," I say to the wildflowers. Soon, when I'm ready, I will say it to Kimberley.

Soon.

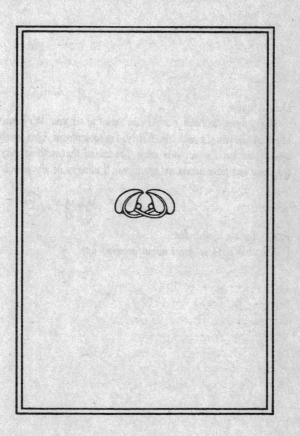

Dear Maggie,

   We're flying to New York! I can't wait to see you! We'll have lunch at Giovanni's and talk. Lately, I'm so confused. I feel lonely and afraid but I'm not sure why. I've learnd that nothing stays the same but promise me, Maggie, you'll always be my freind.

                    xxxx yoyo (ツ)

P.S.   I'm on a new diet.
P.P.S.   What's so great about growing up?

# ABOUT THE AUTHOR

Caryl Brooks was born in New York City and currently lives with her husband on Long Island. She and her husband have three grown children who live near Boston, Massachusetts.

# *point*®

## Other books you will enjoy, about real kids like you!